The Full Moon Rises

A Howl in the Night Book Two

Courtney Rene

Credits
Cover Artist: Designs by Cherith Vaughn
Editor: Kitty Carlisle

Printed in the United States of America

Chapter One

The first day of school was always the same for the first eleven years of my school life. My mom would wake me up with muffins or something special for the first day. She'd do my hair and help me pick out what clothes to wear from the stack of new ones we had purchased just for the occasion of a new year. She'd walk me outside where we'd meet up with my neighbor and best friend, Brian. He and his mom would walk with us to the school or the bus stop, depending on the year. I had Brian at my side making it all easier. The first day of school was no big deal, as long as Brian and I were together.

That scenario would not be the case for me the beginning of my junior year. Everything had changed. I stood up on my own. Picked out my own clothes from the old ones I'd had for a while. There were no new ones. There would be no muffins with my mom or her helping with my hair. Who knew what she was even doing that day. It certainly had nothing to do with me. I know it had been my choice to move away from my home to live with my grandfather, but I'd thought she'd at least still be a part of my life. That she'd want to be involved. Apparently, I was wrong.

Then there was Brian. He and I hadn't spoken in weeks. We wouldn't be going to school together for the first time in all our school years. That was the hardest part for me. I would be starting at a new school full of people that were maybe not strangers, but people I didn't know. He would be going to the same school and with the same people he always had. It was going to be a complicated year for me.

I looked in the mirror at myself in my jeans and t-shirt and didn't really like what I saw. My hair hung long down to almost my waist and was getting longer every day. It so needed a trim. I hadn't bothered with makeup as I still had a nice tan from the summer sun. "Whelp, that's as good as I'm going to get, I guess." I smoothed my hair with one hand as I turned from the mirror and left my room to find something to eat.

The kitchen was down the hall, then down the back stairs. I flounced down the steps and entered the kitchen with as much fake excitement as I could manage, only I shouldn't have even bothered. I was alone. However, on the table in what Peggy, the house help maid person, called the breakfast nook, was a new purple plaid bag. I pulled it toward me and opened it. I wasn't going to pretend it couldn't be for me, as I was the only person under the age of fifty in the house. Let alone the fact that my posh grandfather wouldn't be caught dead with a backpack in purple.

It was stuffed to the seams with school supplies. I couldn't help the smile that blossomed on my face as I looked at the pack of No. 2 pencils, spiral notebooks, and just about anything else I could possibly need for school. I hadn't been forgotten after all.

Yes, it was different, and yes it was not what my mother used to do, but it was something, and it was something nice. I heard someone come up behind me, and I turned to find my grandfather hesitating in the doorway.

I'd been living with him for about two months, and we were not much closer than we were upon our first meeting. I didn't even know what his age was, let alone anything about his history. Then again, I don't think he knew any more about me than I did him.

"Thank you. For the supplies, I mean. It was sweet of you."

He seemed uncomfortable with the thanks. He stood with his hands firmly gripped behind his back and stood straighter than only a moment before. "You are welcome. I hope it is what you will need in order to do a good job in school." Then after a moment he added, "We have a family reputation to uphold. I expect you will do well."

I didn't roll my eyes, and I didn't sigh, but I wanted too. Sometimes the man was a bit of a jerk. However, as I stood there staring at him, trying to think of something to say, I wondered if that was the problem. He didn't know what to say to me any more than I knew how to talk to him. Everything was so…tense and forced. We really needed to work on that if we were going to live together.

I smiled at him and said, "I'm grateful for them. They are exactly what I will need." I took a blueberry muffin from the counter, fresh made, and oh, my God, they were still a little warm. I grabbed the backpack with my free hand and said, "I better get going. I wouldn't want to be late for my first day."

"Alex will be taking you," he said, still standing tall in the doorway. He was neither in the kitchen nor really out of it. It was like he didn't fit in either place.

"Alex? The chauffeur? Umm…are you sure that's necessary?" I asked. The idea of arriving at school in a sleek limo was not a comfortable one. It seemed a little showy, and not the first impression I wanted to make.

"Alex will see you safely to and from school each week," he said. The tone was as strong as his stance. No arguments would be heard apparently. I decided not to push it.

"What about next week, when I start the other school?"

"He will take you then as well, although I have no idea why you insist on this route. One school, one clan should be enough," he said.

3

I tried not to sound too annoyed even though I clearly was. "Grandfather, we have been through this," I said. "I'm not going to choose one clan over the over. I am going to be part of the whole group. We are all family in some form you know. Alternating one week at the Staton school and one week at the Grey's will give me a chance to understand the families, both sides of it. This is my decision. I get that no one likes the idea, and I get that everyone thinks they can tell me what to do, but you can't. Like it or not, this is how it's going to be for right now. Deal with it."

"Watch your tone with me, young lady. You live here in my home…"

"Yes, I do. For now."

We both stared at each other. Lots of words were left unsaid. Neither of us wanted to fight. Not really.

I opened the door and said, "I'll tell Alex I'm ready." Then because I didn't want to leave with us both still mad, I said, "Don't worry, I'm a good student. I promise."

He didn't respond, and I didn't say anything more. I hitched up my pack on my shoulder and left to find my ride.

~ * ~

I should not have been quite so worried about how it would appear with me arriving with a driver and a limo. Apparently, most of the Staton family clan was as showy as my grandfather. The limos of various degrees of black, sleek and shiny, lined the entryway drive of the little school. I tried to count how many when we arrived, but they were coming and going too fast.

"How many kids go to this school?" I asked Alex.

He glanced at me in the rearview mirror. "About fifty."

That was it? I looked at the school. For a school of about fifty children, it was a bit big. It was made of red brick and only one story, but it was sprawling.

I stepped out of the car on my own and slammed the door closed. Everyone on the walkway to the school stared at me. It could have been that I got out without Alex's help, or it could have been because I was the only girl in sight.

I heard the window power down. Alex said, "I'll be out front waiting for you at the end of the day."

I didn't look back, but I did respond, "Okay." I took a page from my grandfather and straightened my back until it hurt, held my head high, and calmly, and maybe a bit slowly with dread, walked into the school. I didn't look left or right or at anyone, but I felt every single pair of eyes on me the whole way.

Once inside, I headed directly to the office. A woman greeted me with a smile that took me by surprise. Most people in the Staton clan didn't smile. Maybe that was because I hadn't met anyone that was female before. Regardless, I found myself smiling back at her. "Hi. I'm Abigail Staton. I'm new this year."

The smile grew wider on her face, and she said, "Yes. I figured. We get so many girls here you know."

She was teasing me. Wait, a Staton clan member knew how to tease? "Yeah. I bet."

She winked then said, "Okay. So I have your schedule set up for you. It's my understanding that you will spend one week at the Griffin Academic Center and then you spend one week at the Slate Center. Although we are separate buildings, our curriculum is the same, so you will be on track without falling behind at either school. The administration at both buildings have agreed to cooperate with each other and will coordinate your scores for one singular grade each quarter."

"Okay."

"You're making waves, Abby."

"I'm not really trying to, but yeah. I guess I am."

She patted my shoulder and said, "That's not a bad thing. At least some of us don't think it is."

I took a guess and asked, "Would that be the female us?"

A wide, showy smile, full of white teeth appeared on her face. "You got it."

That's what I thought. I smiled back and said, "Girl power."

She lowered her voice and said, "Don't get too showy with it. They will bat you down as quickly as possible here. They don't like the idea of girls having any power over them. It's like being back in the eighteen hundreds sometimes. Take it slow, but don't worry. You're not alone here. It may feel like it, but you aren't. Okay?"

"Okay." She handed me my schedule, and I turned to leave. Then I thought of something. "I'm sorry. What's your name?"

She chuckled softly then said, "Mrs. Staton."

Of course it was. When you lived in a male society, just about everyone would have the same last name. Great.

Then she whispered so softly that I almost didn't hear, "Leslie Staton."

After leaving the office, I headed to my first class. It was math, with Mr. Staton, of course, and in room 101. Okay, that didn't sound too hard. Then I glanced further down on my schedule for the day and saw that my next class was, world history with…Mr. Staton, in room 101. Hmm. In fact, all my classes were in room 101 and all of them were with Mr. Staton.

"What the?"

I found my room rather quickly. The school was actually a square. There was a gymnasium/auditorium in the center and all around it were classrooms. There appeared to be two classrooms on each side

6

with a restroom, and that was it aside from the office up front. So there were what, six classrooms? Then again with only fifty kids, how many rooms did you really need?

I stepped inside room 101 and was again the object of attention for the entire room. I quickly counted and found there were seven kids and the teacher in the room. Seven male kids and one male teacher, I should clarify.

All their eyes stared at me, eight pairs of brown eyes, and heads of dark hair ranging in colors from black to dark brown. Yeah, there was a lot of variety. Even if I hadn't been a girl, I would have stood out like a sore thumb with my brownish blondish hair and blue eyes. But heck add in hips and boobs and yeah, it was no wonder everyone was staring.

My heart was beating so fast inside my chest I wondered if they could see it or hear it. I forced a smile and said, "Hi. I believe you were expecting me?"

They should have been. The fight to get into the two schools had been terrific. Everyone in both clans was aware that I was not going to choose one clan school over the other. I was going to go to both. No playing favorite to be used against the other.

Mr. Staton pointed at an empty desk, or maybe I should call it a table. It was flat with a black surface, big enough for two people to work on comfortably. I was given a work area table all to myself. I wondered if there was a reason for that or if it just worked out that way.

I scanned the room to see if I recognized anyone. No. They were all strangers to me. Maybe I had seen them on the night of the non-battle, but I didn't remember a whole lot about the people that had been there other than my father and the boys I had gotten to know from the other clan.

I missed those boys. William, Oscar, Dillon, and Max maybe more than Taylor. He was too serious and grumpy sometimes, but I still missed him. Where were they? Did William go back to school yet? Why hadn't they contacted me since the night where I'd found balance? He couldn't still be mad at me for not going home with him. Could he?

I pushed those thoughts out of my mind as I sat down, all the while still feeling the heavy weight of eight pairs of eyes.

"Let's settle down everyone and get started. We are going to start at the beginning of your book and work through one chapter a week throughout the year." He pointed at a stack of books over by the window that were evidently math textbooks and said, "Everyone come up and get a book. I expect covers on these books by tomorrow. If they are not covered, you will be held after school. No exceptions." He focused his sharp gaze on my face when he said the last part. As if I would expect preferential treatment. Or maybe they expected me to, because of who my grandfather was. Whatever the reason, I was offended.

We all stood up and filed over to the books to get a copy. Heads lifted into the air. Noses drew in breaths deeply. Then eyes snapped at me. I knew what was coming and I was not in the mood. I lifted a hand and said loudly and as firm as I could, "The first one to say I smell, in any way shape or form, I will tear your face off." I turned my eyes on several of the guys in the class to make sure they heard me, and finished with, "I mean it." Then just to prove I was as serious as I made myself out to be, I let a wave of fur come out on my arms and disappear in a showy display of power. "Just so we're clear."

Silence greeted me. No one moved a muscle, not even Mr. Staton. All eyes were still on me. I wanted to shift fully to wolf. At least in wolf form I was strong and wild. In human form, I was weaker than the boys and they knew it. They tried to intimidate me. I held myself at bay and walked slowly back to my seat with my math book in hand. I sat down and opened the book as if interested in its contents.

Mr. Staton finally took control and said, "Get a move on. Get a book and back to your desk. Open to chapter one and read through it. Then do the problems on page six. All of them." People were glancing through the first chapter and we saw that there were sixty-two problems on page six to complete. We all groaned in realization of the workload we were in for.

I pulled out a green spiral from my pack, wrote MATH on the cover, and got to work going through the chapter. I expected Mr. Staton to at least go over it or teach some of the aspects of the lesson, but he didn't. He sat down behind the desk, pulled out a newspaper, and tuned us all out. Wow. He was going to be an awesome teacher. Not.

Fifty-four-ish minutes later, a bell sounded. It was more of a doorbell type sound than the buzzer type sound that I was used to. I'd made it through most of the problems assigned, but still would have to finish the rest that night.

Mr. Staton looked at the clock above the whiteboard and said, "Four minutes people. Get what you need, and get back on time. I want to get started right away."

I put away my work and slid it as a whole to the side of my desk. Since I wasn't sharing with anyone, I had plenty of space. I stood up in the sea of males and left the room. No one spoke to me. They still glanced at me slyly every chance they could, but I pretended not to notice them. I hustled to the restroom marked for girls and closed myself inside. Silence greeted me, along with the scent of bleach. The room was white and pristine, and although the school wasn't what I would characterize as new, the girl's restroom looked like it was.

I washed my hands and put on a bit of lip-gloss, more to pass some time than because I needed it. Then, when I didn't have anything else to do, I walked back to my class. The same class, the same boys, the same teacher. Man, was it going to be a long as hell day.

9

The bell sounded. Mr. Staton stood up and addressed us. "This is World History." He pointed at a new stack of books, and said, "We will be working our way through two books this year. This is your first-semester book. Everyone come and get a textbook, and again, I want it covered before tomorrow."

The same drill followed. We got up, picked out our books, and sat down. Mr. Staton continued to talk as we did so. "Read chapter one, and then complete the review questions at the end."

I opened my book and did as we were told. "Man, this school sucks," I whispered out loud to no one in particular, but it felt good to say something. Mr. Staton resumed his place at the front of the room behind his paper and that was that. He was awful as a teacher. How long had he checked out and not been teaching? He assigned busy work. Then ignored us the rest of the period.

The guy directly in front of me, half turned in his chair and said under his breath, "It will be better tomorrow. Mrs. Smith comes in on Tuesdays."

"Mrs. Smith?" I whispered back, but the boy had turned back around and didn't respond. I checked him out. He was tall. I could tell by the way his legs sprawled out in front of him all the way through the other side of the desk. He was thin. Maybe a bit on the skinny side, and like all the others in the class, he had dark hair. His was long and shaggy around his face though. Maybe it had a slight bit of curl along the edges. I couldn't tell from where I was sitting for sure, but maybe there was a hint of it.

I started to work on the chapter and was thankfully able to finish the review questions at the end before the bell rang. I piled my history stack with my math stack and quickly stood. I stepped in front of the boy that had spoken to me and tried again. "Who is Mrs. Smith?"

He glanced at me then quickly looked down to the floor again.

I tried again, "I don't really bite, you know." Well not in human form anyway.

He didn't look at me, but he did answer. He said, "Mrs. Smith comes in on Tuesdays and Thursdays to teach. Mr. Staton is Mondays and Wednesday."

I waited for more, but that was all he offered willingly. "Okay, so who comes in on Fridays?" Why did I even have to ask that question?

"Mr. Griffin," he said, and that was all. He stepped around me and just about ran out of the room. The boy towered over me by at least two feet and probably outweighed me by eighty pounds, yet he was the scared one. Too weird.

I still didn't even know his name. The school day was not going fantastic. I didn't leave the room. Instead, I just sat at my desk and waited for the next hour of hell to begin. I glanced at my schedule and saw that the next class was Human Studies. What the hell was Human Studies?

Class began. Books were handed out. Assignments were given and another hour was underway. Human Studies was just what it sounded like. Apparently, it was the anatomy side, and as I flipped through the small book, I saw that it also had mental ideas and characteristics of humans.

I tapped the guy in front of me on the shoulder and asked if we would have wolf studies too?

"No," he said.

"No? Why not?" I asked.

"We don't need to study ourselves. We already know all there is to know."

"Yes, you do. You guys don't know half of what we can do," I snapped and flopped back against my seat. "It's no wonder you all are still unbalanced and haven't joined with your wolves," I mumbled. I knew he heard me, though, because he did the quick glance and look away he'd been doing all morning.

I stared at the back of his head for a minute then said, "What is your name?"

"Shawn," he said.

"Shawn what?" I asked.

He looked at me again, but that time in disbelief. "Staton," he said with a hard tone laced in duh.

"This is too weird." Did every single person have the last name of Staton? Really?

Chapter Two

After Human Studies, it was finally lunch period. I followed the crowd of boys to the cafeteria, which was at the front of the building by the office. We filed into a line. I was immediately in a panic. My mother had always taken care of my lunch money account. Did I have an account there? Was there a code I was supposed to have? How was I supposed to pay for my food? I felt my skin roll and my bones ache. I wanted to shift and just run away from the whole day, but I held on. It was only lunch. How bad could it be?

Finally, it was my turn at the food station. "Oh, my God!" It was all thick, bloody meat. It looked to be an almost-raw steak that sat a quarter of an inch deep in bloody red juice. My stomach heaved and I quickly looked further down the line and away from it. There was a small part of me that was a fierce carnivore, but while in human form, my vegetarian side was firmly in control. In addition to the visual massacre of beef, there was corn, peas, and some type of cookie bar. At the end of the line was a crate full of applesauce, yogurt, and milk.

I looked at the lady flopping out still mooing hunks of flesh onto trays and asked, "Do you have any salad or pasta?"

She looked at me like I was an alien. Maybe to her I was. She was used to boys, growing wolfy boys that obviously craved nothing but meat. That was not me. "No," she said.

13

I tried to calm my rolling stomach by thinking of anything else and said, "Okay. I'll just take the veggies then. Nothing else today." I pressed down the line with my plate of corn and green peas. I stopped at the crate and grabbed both an applesauce and a strawberry yogurt. I then slid down the line where I ended at the register and said quietly to the woman manning it, "How do I pay for my lunch? No one told me what I needed to do."

She smiled and said, "Let me see, I should have your code here." She pulled out a hard covered journal type book and flipped a few pages. "Abby, right?"

"Yes."

"It looks like your grandfather supplied your account for you, both here and at SA."

"SA?" I asked.

"Slate Academy," she said. Then, "Your pin number is nine, two, two, seven. You can use the same pin at both schools."

Apparently everyone from office help to cafeteria people knew that I was flipping between the two clan schools. I shouldn't have been surprised, but I was. Considering I didn't think the two clans had anything to do with each other, it was interesting to find out that when it came to schooling, they did.

I keyed in my pin at the register, said a quick "thanks," and then went to find a place to sit. I thought maybe I could weasel my way into a spot next to Shawn, but I didn't see him or he was hiding.

I looked around for a friendly face, just one, but while all morning long everyone felt like staring, at that moment, not one single set of eyes fell on me. My tray full of veggies suddenly felt heavy in my hands. I shuffled over to an empty round table and sat down, alone. It was one thing when you wanted to be alone, but it was a whole other ball game when you felt alone and wanted nothing more than to be invited in.

I stabbed a fork full of peas, but couldn't bring myself to eat. An aching pain began to make its presence known behind my eyes, because having a headache could only make the day so much better.

I tried to wait out the lunch period, but it was lonely and uncomfortable and all there was to do was focus on the growing pain in my head. I dumped my wasted food in the trashcan and decided it would be better to go back to the classroom where I could at least get some of my math work finished.

Just before I was out of earshot, though, I heard someone say, "Why does she smell like that?" I spun around and tried to find the owner of the unanswered question. The room was so quiet I could hear every breath they took. I focused on that sense and listened, hard. I narrowed in on the sound of one heartbeat that was pumping a bit harder, a bit faster than all the others in the room. His back was to me. I stared daggers at him. He had to know it too. He never turned to look in my direction. Though he did hunch over just a little bit more.

After lunch, I had to survive language arts, science, and apparently the last class of the day was going to be phys. ed. Great. That should be fun.

Mr. Staton was as awesome in the afternoon as he had been all morning long. The only difference was that instead of a newspaper, he pulled out his computer and I assume surfed the web and wasted time all afternoon.

Then gym class came around. I expected the usual change of clothes, run around the gymnasium a few times, maybe play a game or, since it was fall, a short quarter of touch football. I was wrong about that too. Surprise.

Instead, we entered into the gym and sat down on the bleachers where a hulk of a man introduced himself as...Mr. Staton. Yes, the school year was going to be quite confusing. He was a Thomas Staton though. He was dark-haired and tall, just like all the other Staton men, but he was bulky and he was built. He was awesome. Not in an 'I want to date you' type of awesome, but he was definitely attractive in more ways than any of the other boys at the school were. He couldn't be that old either; at least he didn't look that old. He had these deep cheeks and dark eyes that you could fall into. I was practically swooning at the man and his chest. Oh, my God, it was a sight to see. Rippled and muscular even with his shirt covering it, there was no secret to be had. Every definition showed right through.

Then I noticed him noticing me, and I realized something. He knew he was gorgeous, and he was flexing. Yes, yes he was. He was flexing his chest so that I could see what he had to offer, as if he were a horse on the market for stud. I wasn't sure what that made me, but all the same it was a bummer. He was going to be just like every other Staton male shapeshifter I'd met. They were either afraid of me as a female or they thought they could own me for the same reason. I knew then what category Mr. Thomas Staton would fall into.

I took a breath and let it out in a loud sigh. It was going to be a very, very long year. Staton men and I just didn't get along, apparently.

Gym didn't get better after my realization. It was not your normal gym class after all. Oh no, that would be too easy.

"Welcome to phys. ed.," Mr. Staton said. "This first quarter you will be graded on your shifting abilities. Is there anyone that is not able to shift yet in this class?"

No one raised a hand.

"Good," he said. "Then we can get started. Put all your belongings on the bleachers and come stand on the red line."

Warning bells were going off in my head, as if it didn't hurt enough all by itself. I was not getting naked in front of eight guys. Not happening. I raised my hand, and when he turned to me, I knew he had been expecting it by the slightly amused expression on his face. "Yeah, that's going to be a problem for me," I said.

16

"Why?" he asked, as if he had no clue.

"Umm…because I'm a girl."

He showed me his teeth in what I believe may have been a smile, but it had a sharp edge to it. "If you don't participate in my class, you will fail. No exceptions. Ever.

Just like a Staton to bully me. I was actually getting used to it and learning how to deal with them. Instead of getting upset and feeling cowed, I got mad. I smiled back at him with the same showing of my teeth, and said, "Fine. I will be sure to discuss this issue with my grandfather. I'm sure he will be very happy to hear you are sexually intimidating his granddaughter. His only shifting granddaughter."

He stared at me. "I am not sexually intimidating you."

I stared right back. "Yes, you are, and you know it. Expecting one girl to undress and be ogled by you and a room full of teenage boys is sexual in nature and intimidating as hell. It's not going to happen. No matter how much you want to see this body of mine, you won't. Ever." I wanted him to know I knew what he was about. I knew who he was and what he was. I didn't care how good looking he was on the outside, he was ugly everywhere else.

The rest of the guys in the class looked between us, waiting to see who would give.

I slowly lifted a negligent shoulder and said, "Maybe you don't actually want this job…" I didn't know if my grandfather would take my side or not, but Mr. Buff-and-bully didn't know that.

"Fine!" he snapped. "Go sit on the bleachers and you can watch."

I smiled. Victorious. I pushed him a little more. I was in a mood anyway after the day I'd had. The ache behind my eyes wasn't helping either. "So…you want me to stare at a bunch of naked teenager boys. Not sure that's a good idea either."

"Get out of my class. Go somewhere, anywhere else. Just get out!" he yelled. The words echoed around the room, he'd screamed so loud.

I hopped up from my seat and skipped out of the room, happy in winning my little battle. I lugged my bag full of books and homework outside, where I intended to wait for my ride. I didn't need to, though, as Alex was already there, along with many other drivers.

"Did you wait out here all day?" I asked when he got out to open my door.

"No," he said and closed my door, effectively ending any further conversation.

We drove straight home. I left the car without waiting for Alex to come around and all but dragged my bag into the house. I headed straight for the kitchen, hoping to find something decent to eat. After having tossed out my lunch, I was starving.

I found my grandfather in the kitchen, seated at the little round wooden table in the nook. "Were you waiting for me?" I asked, a bit of a demand than a question, and a bit hopeful that he was.

"Alex called to let me know you were on your way back," he said. He sat straight-backed and stiff in the chair. He looked out of place even in his own kitchen. He was all old world and classic, and the kitchen was warm and soft and modern.

I dropped my bag beside a chair and headed over to rummage around in the pantry. I grabbed a snack bag of chips and plopped down at the table across from him. When he didn't say anything, I asked, "Was there something you needed?"

"I wondered how your first day of school went," he said.

I tried to see if he was being polite or if he really was interested. "Do you really want to know or do you just want me to say it was great?" I was tired of the day, and I wasn't in the mood to please anyone else.

He didn't answer right away, but he did at least answer me. "I would like your honest thoughts on the school."

Okay, fine. I'd give him my honest thoughts. "No one talked to me. I sat alone all day, even at lunch. Everyone hates me. Mr. Staton, the Glen one, is a total waste in the teacher department. He doesn't teach at all. He gives out assignments and expects us to learn everything and anything ourselves. He sucks."

"First, not everyone hates you," he said.

"Whatever," I replied and crossed my arms over my chest.

"Second, Mr. Staton has been a teacher at that school for twenty years," he said.

I cut him off before he could say anything glowing on behalf of the man. "Yeah, and it shows. He does not want to teach. He is collecting a paycheck. That's it. I hope you aren't paying him very much as I could be a better teacher than that man is. And what is up with Mr. Muscles Staton in the gym. He's an ass."

"Watch yourself, young lady!" he snapped and stood up quickly, knocking the chair back, but not over.

I was a bit unnerved by the burst of anger, but I tried not to show it. Not that I should have been surprised – he was a Staton and full of raw emotion. They all seemed to be. "You said you really wanted to know," I said quietly.

"That is no excuse for acting common and talking like trash," he said as he calmly righted his chair and sat back down.

Did he regret his burst of emotion? Was he trying to actually have a real conversation with me? "You're right. I'm sorry," I said. "Mr. Thomas Staton in the gym was upsetting to me today. It's not your fault, and I should not have taken it out on you."

He nodded his head then asked, "Why was he unacceptable?"

I decided to talk with my grandfather. We had been tiptoeing around each other for weeks. I was living with him in order to form a

19

relationship with him, and that was the first real conversation we'd had in all that time. If he was willing to try, then so was I. "He made me feel dirty. He made me feel like I was just some stupid girl. He actually expected me to take off my clothes in his class in front of everyone and then got mad when I made it into a big deal."

"What do you mean?" he asked. He sounded like he really wanted to know. It confused me. No one ever wanted to hear what I thought anymore.

"It was like, if he could get my clothes away from me, I would be weak in front of them all. He could show all those boys and himself that I was nothing, just some girl. It made me mad. I felt small, and I hate to admit it, but I felt intimidated by him. I refused to take off my clothes and participate in his class."

"What happened then?" he asked.

"He got mad. So, I told him you would be unhappy with his treatment of me."

"I see," he said, drawing out the words ominously.

I tried to wait him out. I tried to let him take it all in. I tried, but in the end I caved and said, "I'm sorry if you're mad at me for bringing your name into it, but I'm not sorry that I didn't take off my clothes. I'm not sorry for telling him what I thought, and I am not sorry that I didn't let him bully me and make me feel like crap about myself and being a girl and ..."

"Abigail, stop," he said as he held out his hand to punctuate his words. "I'm not angry with you. In fact, as strange as it may seem in your eyes, I'm proud of you. I am on your side."

"You are?" I asked. To say I was surprised would be the understatement of the year. I was floored. Not one of the Staton males had ever stood up for me or even pretended to be on my side. Not once.

"Yes, I am," he said. "First, let's discuss your Monday teacher, Mr. Staton."

"And Wednesday."

"Excuse me?" my grandfather asked.

"He's the Monday and Wednesday teacher," I answered.

"Regardless, as I already said, he has been a teacher with the school for over twenty years. Maybe it's time that we did a peer review of Mr. Staton. I can't imagine the rest of the children are enjoying their time with him any more than you are. The other instructors may not be aware of his…methods. I will contact the schoolboard."

"Okay, I'm good with that. What about Mr. Testosterone?" I asked.

"Him, I think I will deal with myself. However," he said and paused to make sure I was paying attention, "We have not had females in the school for many years now. This may be too much of a change for Mr. Thomas Staton."

"It was more than that, though," I said.

"I am aware that it probably was. I know Thomas. He is a bit of a peacock. However, I can't accuse him of inappropriate behavior just on your word. I believe you, that's not the issue," he said.

I knew what the issue was. It was a male-versus-female issue. In the world of wolves and shifters, females were weak and under the care and keeping of the big strong men. Females were breeding material and, to put it mildly, house slaves.

Some would have said it was love and caring. I wasn't sure if I believed in love for the male wolves. Maybe they did. Maybe it was just a different type of love, but after seeing the control my father had over my mother, it wasn't something I was interested in. Then again, it could be because my mother was just a human, an outsider that he felt he needed to be in firm control. Whereas I was a wolf shifter – maybe it would be different for me. Maybe, but I doubted it. I had a feeling it was females in general that the males thought they needed to control.

I turned my mind away from thoughts of my mother. It was still a very touchy issue with me. I shoved her to the back recesses of my mind and concentrated on the problem at hand. "So what do we do about gym class?"

"My understanding is that you need a full two semesters of physical education in order to graduate. That is the state standard, correct?"

"Yes," I said following his line of thought happily. "And I have already completed my two semesters through the public school system."

"Exactly. While I am discussing teachers' credentials with the schoolboard, I should be able to have you moved to a study session while the others in your class complete their gym training credits."

Problem solved, for the moment anyway. Who knew what problems would come up the rest of the week or, worse yet, next week at the Slate school.

"Now, onto another issue," my grandfather said. He seemed too nonchalant about it, too calm in his tone. I was immediately put on guard.

"Okay, what is the other issue?" I asked.

"You mother and father," he said. He said it as if it was no big deal, when we both knew darn well that it was a very big deal.

"What about them?" I kept my tone calm and neutral, but I felt my heart quicken and I immediately wanted to shift to wolf in order to protect myself from the emotion that always forced its way out whenever anything had to do with my mother and father.

"When are you next going over to their house?" he asked.

My house! It was my house too! In fact, it was my house before it was his house. I felt and saw brown fur ripple its way over my skin before slipping back out of sight. I took a slow breath. Then I did it again. Trying in vain to calm down.

My grandfather pretended he didn't see my struggles. Was that good, in that he was trying to give me privacy with my out-in-the-open emotions; or was it bad, in that he didn't care whether I was upset or not?

"You can't run from them forever," he said.

Oh, yes I could. "I'm not running," I said.

"You haven't been to the house in weeks. The last time you were there was to pack up a few of your belongings to come live here."

"So," I snapped.

"So, don't you still have some items at the house you would like to get? Don't you want to see your mother and father?"

I narrowed my eyes at him. Why was he pushing me on the issue? Why now, when he had not said a single word about it before? What was he hiding? I stared at him.

"What?" I asked. Maybe asked is not quite right. It was more of a snarl, more menacing than a simple word would appear.

"They have news for you, Abigail," he said pressing forward with his own agenda.

I didn't want to hear any more. I stood up, my bag already in my hand and said, "I'll go over tomorrow after school. I have too much work today to do it." I held up my overflowing bag as if it were proof of the workload.

He held my eyes with his own and said, "Do you promise?"

I wanted to lie. I wanted to promise then forget all about it tomorrow. I wanted to pretend it was no big deal. I didn't do any of that. For some reason, I knew he would know if I lied. He had some kind of sixth sense when it came to lies. "I promise. I'll go tomorrow."

He got to his feet, brushed off his black slacks, and stood tall before me. The white of his hair caught my eye. How old was he? "Good. I'm glad we could discuss this like adults."

"Sure." I still wondered about the man I really knew nothing about. "Can I ask you something?"

"Yes," he replied.

"When is your birthday?"

He seemed surprised by my question, but then a grin appeared on his face for only a moment before his face resumed the bored mask of indifference he tended to wear. "December second," he answered.

He didn't give me a year, and I was too afraid to push my luck and ask right then. However, it was something. "Okay. Thanks."

He didn't ask why I wanted to know, and I didn't push for more. We were making headway, at least.

I turned to go to my room and said over my shoulder, just before I began my climb up the back staircase, "We really need to discuss the décor of the house. It's so depressing."

I swear I heard him chuckle. Maybe it was only what I wanted to hear, but I could swear he did.

Chapter Three

Alex was ready and waiting for me the next morning, as he had been the day before. "Morning," I said trying to cheer myself as well as be friendly to him as I sat down in the car.

"Good morning, Ms. Abigail," he said as he shut the door.

"It's just Abby," I said to the closed door, even though I knew he couldn't hear me. I gave up making friends with Alex for the moment. There was no real reason to try other than to make my interactions with him feel less awkward.

Once at school, I quickly walked to my class and sat down alone, at the back of the room. I set out the morning's books and notebooks in the space next to me and waited for the long day to begin. The boys began to file in. "Stop it," I snapped when I couldn't take it anymore.

"Stop what," Shawn said as he came into the room.

"Smelling me," I growled. Each one of the boys had walked next to me and taken in a deep long smelling breath. It was hard to miss the sound of air pulling noisily through their noses.

A feminine laugh came from the back of the room. I snapped my head around and saw a very pretty, not too old, woman walk into the room. She was dressed in jeans. Granted she had on a nice black sweater to class it up, but she was in jeans all the same. I liked her right off.

"Oh, that. They can't help it," she said.

It was my turn to be confused. "Help what?" I asked her.

"You smell like," she said and lifted her eyes up to the ceiling as if in deep thought then said, "chocolate and caramel sauce over a fresh from the oven brownie. Or so I have been told."

She rested her hand on my shoulder and bent down to loudly whisper, "So they can't help but take in your lovely scent." Then in a normal tone she said, "Welcome to the school. It's about time we had some female DNA around here to mix it up a little bit."

She continued her way up front where she perched on the corner of the desk. "So, what did you get to read yesterday and what was your homework?"

Hands shot up into the air and, as they say, the day was off and running. She engaged us. She taught us. She was as awesome as she sounded only even better than I had hoped. When the lunch hour bell rang, I was shocked at how quickly the day had gone.

I left the room with little hope of what was to be served for lunch. While waiting in line, I was not surprised to see trays of meat awaiting me. I didn't focus on that, though. Instead when it was my turn, I asked, "What do I need to do to get a salad?"

"Bring it in yourself," Mrs. Smith said from behind me.

I smiled at her with complete understanding. "That's what I was afraid of."

"You get used to it," she said craning around me to look at what was being served. "Look they have nice steamed broccoli today, and oooh look, rice cereal treats!"

"I'll take a bowl of the veggies and a cereal bar thing," I said to the cafeteria woman, the same one that I had seen the day before.

She scooped up my requested items, handed them over to me. She then surprised me when she said, "I put in an order for salad and pasta dishes. They should be here by the time you get back from your off week at the other school."

"Really?" I was happier at the prospect than you would expect.

"Yep. I got you covered, hon," she said and winked.

"Wow," Mrs. Smith said. "You must be something special. I've been trying to get something other than meat, meat, and more meat here for years."

I didn't want her to think of me as special any more than I wanted to be. I wanted to be normal. "Nah. I just whined," I said and smiled innocently.

I entered the cafeteria and was again stuck with the problem of finding a place to sit. I didn't want to sit alone again. I needed to figure out a way to break into the boys groups. Somehow. I zeroed in on a group of four boys that I thought sat up toward the front in my classes. From the back, I could have picked them out easily, as that was all I stared at all day long. From the front, though, I wasn't too sure.

I braved up and sauntered over to the table. I didn't ask to sit down. I just did, plunking my tray down at the same time. "Hey," I said with as much cheer as I could muster. "Thought I'd join you guys. I'm sure you don't mind. It's an easy way to do a meet and greet without all the school subjects getting in the way."

I rambled on a bit. I didn't want to give any of them a chance to ask what the hell I thought I was doing sitting at their table. I stabbed a broccoli tree with my fork and shoved it in my mouth, and continued to talk around the food in my cheeks. "I have to say I am enjoying this day's classes a whole heck of a lot more than yesterday's. Is it just me or was yesterday bad?"

I allowed a moment for someone to respond. They didn't. They did, however, stare, and stare quite hard at me. They didn't eat. They didn't move a muscle, other than to breathe.

"You guys all right?" I asked. I used my fork to point at their trays and said, "You going to eat? It's getting cold."

Still nothing. "Okay." I said and shoved another forkful into my mouth. While I chewed, I wracked my brain for an idea, any idea, to get them to talk to me. I had nothing. No ideas at all, which frustrated me to no end. "Fine," I snapped. "What do I have to do to get you guys to talk to me? Geez!"

One of the guys made honest to God eye contact with me and said, "Will you answer a question for me, without getting mad?"

I pondered his question. Was I willing to go that route and open the door to any question in the world? "You can ask, and I will do my best to not get mad, but I can't promise you."

"Can you really shift single parts? Can you shift whenever you want and whenever you don't want?"

That was two questions, but they were easy. "Yes, to both." I pulled up the sleeve of my shirt and allowed my forearm and hand to shift to a foreleg and paw of a wolf. The rest of me stayed the same. It wasn't taxing. It wasn't hard. I thought about it, and I changed.

"Wow!" he said.

I shrugged.

"Can I ask you something else?"

"You have to tell me your names first," I said.

"I'm JJ, this is Jack," he said to the boy at his side, "and that is Bruce, and you know Shawn," he said going around the table.

I took in their faces and their characteristics so that I could keep them straight in my mind. It wasn't easy since they all had dark hair, dark eyes, and were tall. However, Shawn was more skinny and lanky. JJ was a bit thick around the middle. Jack had these bushman eyebrows that were hard to not stare at. Then there was Bruce. The only thing I could pick out to distinguish him was that his face was softer than the others. Not weak or feminine, but softer bones in his cheeks, smaller lips and nose, and a rounded chin. "Okay, JJ, what's your question?"

"Is it true your mom is a human?" he asked.

28

I hesitated. I wasn't sure if I wanted to discuss my odd family life. Then I figured what the hell. No one cared about how I felt about it anyway, so it must not be that big of a deal. "Yes. She's full human."

"Then how come you are a girl and can shift?" Shawn asked, finally joining the conversation.

"No idea," I asked. I wasn't lying or evading; I really didn't have a clue.

"How come we never heard of you until a few months ago?" Jack asked.

"Because I didn't know about me or the wolves or the clans until then. I didn't even know such a thing could exist," I said.

"But how can you be a girl and shift?" JJ asked again. "There has to be a reason, right? You aren't even full-blooded."

I almost choked on my rice cereal treat. The way he'd said it, sounded like an insult. "Hey," I snapped. "I'm pretty sure none of us is full-blooded. Aren't your moms just plain ole humans too? Can't you shift? What makes you any better than me? It's not that Y chromosome that's for sure."

Bruce leaned over the table and said with quiet authority, "I don't think that's quite what he meant."

"Then what did you mean, JJ?" I asked.

"I mean, why are you any more special than us? You're just a girl," he said.

"That didn't help, JJ," Bruce said.

"Yeah, not good," Jack said.

"Geez, JJ," Shawn said.

I tried to not be offended. I really did, but I couldn't help it. "Just a girl?" All four faces in different arrays of guilt faced me. "Whelp, this has been informative." I gathered up my trash and tray. "I'll see you in class, boys." I stood up and left them at their table

"Just a girl? Really?" I said out loud to the empty hallway on my way back to class.

The afternoon began and finished without incident other than a few strange looks from my lunch period friends and one or two from Mrs. Smith. When it was time to go to gym, I poked around as long as I could before entering the gymnasium. I needn't have worried. I barely made it two steps inside the door before Mr. Staton barked at me that I was excused from his class until further notice. I was dismissed for the day. Yay!

I skipped out of school to the car, where Alex was waiting for me. "I've been told you are going home this afternoon to visit your family?"

It was said as a question but also a statement that didn't need a reply. I gave him one anyway. "Sure," I said and quickly hopped in.

It wasn't a long drive to my house. I remembered the first time I made the trip from my house to my grandfather's. It had felt like it took forever, but in reality, it was only on the other side of town.

I got out on my own. I secretly wondered if that annoyed Alex. I hadn't even made it up to the door when I heard my name being called. I turned and saw Brian, my neighbor and one-time best friend, coming up the driveway.

"Hey," I said, very happy to see a friendly face.

"Hey. Where have you been?" he asked.

I shrugged. Brian was not one of the wolves and we weren't all that great of friends anymore, so there wasn't much I could tell him.

"I miss you at school," he said.

"Yeah, I know what you mean."

"The first day, our routine, it was weird without you," he said.

"It was definitely different this year."

"Why was that? Where did you go?" he asked.

What to say, what to say? "Things are...weird here. I've been staying with my grandfather, and they all thought it would be nice if I went to the private school they all went to. Carry on the family tradition, you know?" It was sort of true.

"Now that you have money you mean," he said.

"No, I don't have anything," I snapped back at him. "I have to go. I'll see you later," I said and turned to go inside.

"Wait," he said.

I turned back and waited.

"I wanted to talk to you about a group I met. You may be interested in their cause." He wasn't looking at me as he talked but off to the side of where I stood. I stepped into the range of his vision and he quickly looked down. What was that all about? Why wouldn't he look at me? Something was off. I didn't now what it was, though. I felt it under my skin, just a little tingly feeling of awareness.

"What is their cause?" I asked.

"I can set up a meeting," he rushed out. "They can tell you all about it themselves."

Yeah, something wasn't right. He seemed anxious and a bit desperate. I shook my head and said, "No, not right now."

"When? Tomorrow?"

I again shook my head then said, "No, not tomorrow. Look, I have to go. I'll see you soon." I didn't give him a chance to respond or say anything more. I turned and rushed away from him. My day had been long enough and I still had to deal with my mother and my father. I didn't feel like trying to deal with Brian too.

I stepped up to the door and stopped. Was I supposed to knock? Did I just go in? I didn't have to figure it out as Derek opened the door for me and stepped aside to let me through. He stepped back just enough that I could get in but not enough that I could get in without brushing against him on my way past.

31

Derek and I'd had a rocky start upon meeting for the first time. My dad wanted him to be my mate. Hand-picked him for me. I had other ideas. I wanted to mate or get married for love, not for good breeding. Yuck. Derek, I couldn't tell what he really wanted. Oh, he wanted to please my family, my father in particular, but what else? He didn't even believe in love. He liked the idea of me, but that wouldn't be enough. Not for me anyway. Even knowing all that, there was something about that guy that pulled me in, all the while there was something that pushed me away.

He was gorgeous. I don't mean he was okay. I mean he was so nice to look at that there were moments when he was in front of me that I couldn't help myself but stare at him. His wide, strong chest...man was it lovely. His dark piercing eyes pulled me in. There was also something in the air, some male pheromone or something that made my heart beat fast and my legs go all weak.

Then he opened him mouth and I was good to go.

"Looking good, Abby," he drawled and took a long slow look from my head to my toes, leaving me feeling a little dirty.

"Jerk," I said as I moved past him.

"Bitch," he said right back, followed by a hearty laugh. His word didn't have any heat to it, any more than mine had. It was almost a game between us. I hated him. He wanted me. It was all good.

I wanted to ask where my mother was to try to avoid what I knew was coming, but apparently that was not going to be the case, as my father silhouetted the doorway from the front room to the kitchen. "Come in, Abby. I was just having a snack. Are you hungry?" he asked.

"No," I said, but I did head into the kitchen. It was a familiar spot, one that brought back memories, mainly good – a few bad. It was a comfortable room. I sat down at the table and said, "So, how is everything."

"Good," he said.

I drummed my fingers on the table and tried again. "So, where's mom?"

"You mother is not feeling well this afternoon. She is lying down."

"Why? What's the matter with her? She's never sick." A small burst of alarm made its way into my brain.

"Nothing is the matter with her – she's with child."

The bomb dropped just like that on my unsuspecting heart and had me silenced as easily as anything could have.

"We hope you will be happy for us."

Happy? Was he kidding? He sat down in the chair across from me and tried another tactic. "This is the fresh start we wanted."

"She's too old to be having babies," I said.

"Thirty-seven is not too old," he replied.

I had nothing else to say. I sat there silent. My father did the same. The room was very heavy with unspoken emotions. Uncomfortable even.

"Do you have nothing else to say to me?" he asked.

"What do you want me to say?" I asked.

"Well, you could start with congratulations."

"Congratulations," I replied. The tone was so deadpan and empty of emotion he couldn't have missed the sarcasm it screamed.

A low growl rumbled in his chest. I tried not to be intimidated. I was just as much wolf as he was. In fact I should be stronger because I was balanced within, and he was not. He was still part wolf and part human, and he didn't have control as I did. However, that very reason was also why I was a bit afraid.

All of us wolf shifters started out as two entities basically fighting over one body. I was the oddball in the entire species that instead of fighting a continual battle with the wolf inside me, we blended together to form one single entity. I was the only one to have accomplished this…so far. I hoped to get others to reach this form of balance with their wolves, but so far, no luck.

He slammed the palm of his hand down on the table so hard it shook under the abuse. "Why can't you be happy for us?" he demanded.

"Because in making yourselves happy you are trying to erase me!" I yelled right back at him. Apparently I didn't have as much control over myself as I thought I did.

"We deserve a fresh start, a new beginning," he said.

"That's exactly what I'm talking about. You want a beginning, but you are forgetting your past. I'm your past. I was your beginning and you threw me away, and she is throwing me away now. How do you expect me to be happy about that?" I was trying to stay in my seat, but I wanted to jump up and pace about the room. I needed to move.

"We are starting a family," he said.

"No, you aren't starting one. You are continuing one," I said. Why couldn't they see how much their words hurt me? I was the start of their family. Did they forget that? Did he?

We stared at each other in silence, my blue eyes to his almost black. When I couldn't take it anymore, I got to my feet and said, "Well this has been fun, but I need to get home."

I walked passed him and almost made it out of the room before his words stopped me in my tracks. "One more thing before you go. We need you to get the rest of your things out of your room. We want to turn it into a nursery."

My eyes burned at his cold, unfeeling words. There was my answer. No, they had no idea or simply didn't care that they were tearing me apart on the inside. Wiping me out of their lives and now wiping me out of my own home. "Fine. I'll come back tomorrow to get my possessions."

"Don't forget," he said.

I said over my shoulder, not even bothering to give him my attention, "I'd like to forget you."

I walked out into the sunshine, what was left of it anyway. I tilted my face toward the harsh orange light and tried not to cry. I felt sad. Inside my soul, I felt sad. I was beginning a new stage in my life, but I was losing my past because of it. My home, my friends, my mother. Why was it so hard?

"Abby! Stop!" Derek said. He'd come out the door and was stalking down the steps toward me.

He was so overdramatic. I wasn't running away. In fact, I wasn't running anywhere. I was standing in the driveway. "What do you want, Derek?"

"You don't understand the mess you always leave behind, do you?" he asked.

"What are you talking about?"

"Every time you come here, you leave the house in an upheaval. Why do you make everything into such a big deal?"

"Me? You're blaming me for everything?" I was incredulous. "This is none of your business. He is not your dad. She is not your mother. They are mine!" I was yelling at him by then, not even bothering to keep my voice down. "But they don't give a shit about that. They don't give a crap about me at all. In fact, all they want is me and my junk out of their house and out of their lives so they can start a real family." I was so angry I wanted to tear him apart just because he was the one standing there.

"Don't be a baby," he said.

"You know what? Piss off." I turned away from him to end the conversation.

He grabbed my elbow hard and yanked me back around to face him. I saw red. At that moment, I was furious at everyone. I swung around and with as much power and anger and fury as I could pull from within my body, I smacked him full in the face. "Let go of me!" I shrieked.

My teeth suddenly hurt as my face began to lengthen. A set of long canines shot through my gums, forcing their way forward. I growled in warning that I was at my limit and was about to go wolf.

Derek didn't appear to be afraid. He jerked me forward until my face was almost touching his. He didn't say anything. Instead, he growled deep and menacing in his chest. It was a showdown, only I wasn't sure of what type.

I allowed my face to return to normal, but I stayed right there in his and growled back. I wasn't in the mood to be intimated. He pulled me in closer, causing our noses to touch.

I held my breath and waited to see what he would do next. I'd like to pretend that I was surprised when he let out the breath he was holding, leaned in, and devoured me in the hottest kiss I'd ever had, but I wasn't.

There was a part of me that wanted it. The ramped up tension, the anger, it was all foreplay. There was still a part of me that wanted him. It wasn't rational and it wasn't sane, but it was there and it was front and center.

I buried both my hands into his long thick hair and held him to me. I let him take control as he nipped at my lips and then thrust his tongue into my mouth. When he'd kissed me in the past, I was able to blame the wolf on my own lust. I couldn't do that anymore. The wolf was me and I wanted his mouth on mine. I wanted to breathe him in. He growled into my mouth and pressed my body full against his. I was drowning in him and loving it.

"Ahem."

An unsubtle cough penetrated my lust-fueled brain not a moment too soon. I pulled back in shock at my actions and in disappointment that the moment ended. I stared at Derek and saw the same expression mirrored on his face.

36

I slowly turned my head in the direction of the noise and saw to my shock and maybe a little embarrassment Brian's red-cheeked face. He was either embarrassed as well or...I sniffed the air and realized he was angry. The emotion was thick in the air.

Why? Brian and I weren't a thing. Yeah, he'd wanted to be, but I didn't see him like that at all. I'd made that very clear to him in the past.

I stepped away from Derek. I looked at him and then at Brian. I weaseled out of trying to come up with an explanation and decided retreat was a better option. I walked to the limo, sat down, and told Alex, "Let's go," and left them all behind. I'd deal with them later. I refused to think of either issue at the moment. Maybe tomorrow.

Chapter Four

By the time I arrived home, it was getting dark. I walked inside, dropped my bag in the foyer, and headed toward the back of the house with the intent of going right out the back door. I almost made it too, but my grandfather stopped me just before I was able to slip out.

"Where you going?"

"I need a run," I said. "I need time to think, and a run always works out some of my energy and tension."

"You want company?" he asked.

He wanted to come with me? Really? "Sure, why not?" I said and continued out the door. I shifted directly into wolf form. My body exploded with soft brown fur. My back arched me down to all fours. My face lengthened while my hands and feet curled into paws and claws. One moment I was a young teenage girl, the next, I was full wolf. I didn't give the slightest thought to the destruction of my clothes. I just wanted to run.

I paced in a small circle while I waited for my grandfather. I'd never actually seen him in wolf form. I was surprised when he appeared since he didn't look old like I expected. No, he looked strong and fierce. His muzzle and around his eyes had a bit more white threaded throughout, but the rest of him was dark brown with whirls of black while I was a light brown solid color almost from head to toe.

His eyes were the same dark brown in both forms whereas mine were darker, deeper when in the form of the wolf.

I chuffed a short barking sound at him as a sort of confirmation of whether or not he was ready. He merely lifted his head in a nod of assent. That was all the confirmation I needed. I turned and ran through the flat grassy yard and onward to the forest.

The moment I entered the trees, I felt my tense muscles due to the stress of my day finally began to relax. They warmed with my exertion and carried me onward. My senses overloaded with information. The trees were slowly drifting to sleep for the winter. Leaves were dropping and spoiling on the ground. The scent of the rodents hiding in the forest and the sounds they screamed to warn of my coming. I loved the forest. It was home to me. Not just while in wolf form, but whenever I could escape into it, it always welcomed me in. There was nothing to fear in the forest, not for me anyway.

I stopped at a clear stream and lapped at the cold water. The brown wolf appeared at my side. Neither of us was out of breath, nor were we ready to go back. I waited until he had his fill from the stream and then I took off again.

I was happy. The sound of our paws hitting the ground was comforting and just what my body and soul needed. After a while, I finally turned us back and headed toward the house. I could stay out all night, but that wasn't the way things were. I had to go back. I couldn't run from the world forever, no matter how tempting it may be. There was a time I considered it. I won't deny it.

When we arrived back at the house, I wasn't certain how to go forward. I couldn't just shift back into human form and I certainly didn't want my grandfather to either. There are some naked things I never ever wanted to see, and my grandfather was one of them.

I stayed back and let him take the lead. He stepped up to the door and pawed at it once, twice. The door opened almost immediately, as if someone had been waiting for us. It was the housekeeper. She smiled at our appearance and pushed the door wide to let us in. My grandfather nodded his long head at her in appreciation as he passed through the room. I brushed my tail against her legs in my own show of affection and then padded up the back steps to my room where I changed back into my human form in private.

After getting dressed in PJs for the night, I flopped down on my bed. That was just what I needed. I felt better and ready to take on the world again.

~ * ~

I dropped my tray of steamed veggies and what looked like a no-bake cookie down at the table with my four new friends. 'Friends' was maybe not the right word. They all looked like I was keeping them hostage with my presence, but I was not giving up. What was it going to take to make friends out of the Staton men?

"Well, the morning was as much a waste as Monday's was. Mr. Staton should not be teaching." No one agreed or disagreed, and I wasn't even sure if they were breathing. I tried a different tactic. "So, what's the story with Mrs. Smith? How does a regular person get to teach at this school?"

"She's not exactly regular," Shawn said.

Finally! Someone was talking back. Holding a conversation all by yourself is not easy. "What do you mean?"

"She's married to a Staton," he said.

"But her last name is Smith," I said.

"Yeah, she kept her last name," JJ said. "It was a huge thing when it happened."

"Do they have any kids?" I prodded.

"Yeah, they have two boys. Neither is old enough to shift yet, though. I think the oldest is in the younger class."

I hoped the younger group had better teachers than we had. The table discussion faltered again after that. I was trying to think of something more to talk about, but nothing was coming to mind.

Thankfully, Jack decided to take pity on me or he just finally had something to say. "So are you coming to the full moon party?"

"What's a full moon party?" I asked.

"Well, since we are all forced into the change on the first night of the full moon each month, we have a party together to celebrate. We have a bonfire at sunset. Then when the moon rises and we change, we run the woods and play wolf games. Haven't you ever gone to one before?"

"Nah she was hanging with the others, I bet," JJ said.

"Actually, no," I said. I'd been a shifter for about two months going on three. So, I'd been around for at least two full moons. I'd never been forced into a change due to the moon, though. "I don't change with the moon," I finally said or admitted. I felt guilty saying the words, as if I should be ashamed of something, but I wasn't sure of what.

Their eyes rounded and JJ said, "Why not?"

I shrugged. "I don't know."

"Maybe you just don't realize it's the moon making you change," Jack said.

Yeah, Jack was a bit of an ass. "No, I am aware of when I change and I change when I want to and not any other time." Why was I not connected to the moon like everyone else?

"Wait. I'm the only balanced wolf. I bet that's why I don't have to shift with the moon like the rest of you. It's part of your cursed existence. Until you join with the wolves, you will be out of control with the moon too. That's the only explanation I can think of."

I was making wild assumptions, but it made sense to me. I could tell they were all thinking about it, but it was Bruce that decided to challenge me. "I bet it's because she's a girl."

Sadly, the other boys at the table decided to agree with that theory over mine. "Yeah, that's got to be it," JJ said. "Girls are different."

"Like any of you would know. You don't even know any girl wolves besides me," I said. "Don't act like you are the source of all things female wolf. If anyone is, that would be me."

However, they did have a slight point. I didn't even know all there was to know about me yet. I really wished there were other shifter girls to talk to. I had some questions that were weighing in on my mind.

~ * ~

"Will you be needing any assistance, Miss?" Alex asked.

I stood outside my parents' house with an armload of flat empty boxes. "Not yet, Alex, but thanks. I may need help carrying stuff out, though. You sure you don't mind waiting?"

"No. It's my job, Miss."

"Abby?"

I let out an annoyed breath and prayed for patience as I turned to face Brian. "Haven't seen you in weeks and now I seem to be running into you all the time," I said a bit tersely. I wasn't in the mood for his drama. Ever since I'd told him I wasn't into him 'that way,' we hadn't been on the best of terms. He apparently didn't like the idea of me telling him no. It seemed like I was suddenly running into that quite a bit.

"I saw you and the boxes and thought I'd come see if you needed any help," he said.

Everyone suddenly wanted to be helpful. "No, I'm good," I said shuffling the boxes up higher in my arms. They weren't heavy, but they were awkward to carry.

Brian looked around as if to make sure we were alone. He said, "Your house seems to have an awful lot of dogs lately. Have you noticed?"

"No." A warm flush spread throughout my body. A little streak of worry niggled my brain. "I'm not around here very much if you haven't noticed."

"It just seems weird that I always see them leaving but never actually coming. Don't you think that's strange?" he asked a little more direct.

"No, I don't. They could come in from the woods in the back and go out through the front. I don't know, Brian. What's the big deal? Why are you watching my house anyway?"

He shrugged as if he was trying to appear like he didn't care, but in fact he did. "I'm not, really. I just have been noticing. You know?"

No, I didn't know.

"Did you think about what we were talking about yesterday? The people I met? Their cause?" He asked.

No, I hadn't actually. "Look, Brian. I need to go pack up some of my things. I'll have to talk to you later. Okay?"

"Yeah, sure. Later," he said.

I left him there in the drive and headed for the house. The little hairs on the back of my neck standing at attention told me Brian watched me the whole way. I saw my dad and Derek in the living room when I stepped inside. "Good, you're both here. Wait, don't you guys ever work? You know what, I don't care. Look, all of the in and out wolves are drawing attention from the mere mortals of the block. You need to pay attention to that stuff out here, unless you want to let the world know what you are."

"What *we* are," my father said.

Always had to be contradictory, didn't he. I rolled my eyes at him. "Whatever, deal with it."

I left them murmuring together in the living room while I walked up to my room. I peeked into my mom's room and saw her asleep on the bed. Why was she home? She was all wrapped up in a colorful quilt, huddled tightly under it. I started to step in to check on her, but then I hesitated. Why bother? She got what she wanted. Still, it was hard not to care even with all that had happened. I stepped over to the bed and brushed her hair out of her face. She was burning up with fever.

I heard the floor creak behind me. I turned to find my father waving furiously at me to come to him. I slipped from the room on silent feet to where he stood. "She's got a fever."

"It's not a fever. It's pregnancy," he said matter-of-factly.

"No, she has a fever. She's burning up," I said. "You need to call the doctor."

"All non-wolves run high fevers when carrying wolf babies. She is fine."

"Since when are you the authority on pregnancy?" I asked. What was with wolf men thinking they knew all there was to know about girls and now pregnancy.

"We are a small community. We take care of each other. She is fine," he said.

"Fine." I stomped into my room, but before I closed the door I said, "Can you at least pretend to care about her? Thanks."

I leaned up against the door that I'd basically just slammed in my father's face. My room was not what I expected. I don't know why I thought it would remain untouched in my absence, but seeing it dismantled was hard to take in. My bed was gone. My dresser was too, but that wasn't surprising since I'd cleaned out all my clothes several weeks ago. The bookshelves were still full, though, and my desk was cluttered and packed with memories.

I set up two boxes on the floor by the door. I filled the first one with books. As many as I could cram in, I did. Then, I put in my awards and trophies along with my photos and possessions from within the desk. In the other, I put the quilt that had been on my bed but I found folded up on the floor by the window. Then I turned back to the shelves. My eyes fell on the music boxes. The only gifts I'd ever been given by my father. One was broken thanks to my temper. The glass globe was missing. Even in that shape, the box was still beautiful. The three little pigs and a wolf figures within were still pristine.

I then ran my finger over the globe of one with Little Red Riding Hood. Too bad I saw the gifts for what they were, which was a bribe for my mother more than a gift to me. I packed them up anyway, along with the other knick-knacks. I turned in the empty space and realized everything really was changing, and there was nothing I could do about it. I could either be taken along for the ride or I could take charge of it.

I left the boxes where they sat and went to get Alex to carry them out for me. He'd offered after all.

I said a terse goodbye to my father and Derek and left once again for my grandfather's home. It really was home now. I wasn't needed at my mom's house. My father took over that.

When I arrived at Grandfather's house, I walked inside and really looked around. My grandfather came out to greet me.

"So how'd it go?" he asked.

"Fine. Alex's bringing in my stuff."

"That's not quite what I meant," he said.

I knew that. I just didn't want to discuss it anymore. I'd had the drive back to the house to think and I was tired of the thoughts. "Have you ever thought about redecorating?" I asked.

"No, why would I?" he said.

"Because it's dreary as hell."

"Abigail," he said. "Language."

"I'm serious. You should think about it. Since I'm going to be living here with you, we could do it together. It'd be fun."

He looked around the entryway. It was all dark wood and dim lights. I was sure he saw it like I did: old, ugly, and dark.

"No," he said and left me standing there all by myself.

"Can you at least think about it," I yelled after him.

He didn't say anything, but he did growl at me. "Well, it wasn't a no," I said to no one. I sighed, and the sound echoed off the gloomy walls and bounced back at me.

The door opened and crashed into me from behind. I grabbed the door before it could then slam into the wall. "What the hell?"

"Excuse me, Miss," Alex said as he walked in and up the front stairs carrying one of my boxes. "I'll just set these outside your door. Yes?"

"Yes, fine." At least I had my things. Maybe they would make me feel better. Make my room feel more like my own instead of borrowed.

Chapter Five

The rest of the week raced by without too much excitement. Alex took me to school. No one spoke to me until lunchtime, when the four boys I had attached myself to would say a few words, but all in all, I was lonely.

Saturday arrived, and I was actually looking forward to the full moon party. We were all meeting at my grandfather's house in the clearing just outside the forest. I was dressed in easy-on-and-off clothes consisting of black leggings and a tank top.

I slid on my black flip-flops and headed out back. Several men had gathered wood for a bonfire, and it was already going by the time I arrived. It lit the way with an orange glow that drew people toward it like flies. Everyone was loud and excited.

I expected the boys from school to attend, but it looked like it was everyone in the Staton Clan that I had ever seen and more had also shown up. Young boys that I was pretty sure couldn't even shift were there. The older men of the families sat in chairs around the fire, talking and laughing with their friends and families. The only thing missing was girls. There were none. I was the only one, and I was remarkably uncomfortable.

I spied Derek across the flames and slipped over to his side. "Where are all the ladies?

"Only shifters are allowed," he said.

I pointed to the group of younger boys running wild around the clearing and said, "What about them? They don't shift yet."

"But they will, so they're allowed," he said. "You smell good."

I decided to accept the compliment instead of chaffing at it for once. "Thanks."

He leaned down and ran his face over my neck and inhaled. "Really good," he said a growl rumbling in his chest.

"Hey," I snapped and jerked back a few steps from him. "Cut it out."

His eyes bore into me. They were intense and steely. I felt my breath catch in my lungs at the heat in his eyes, but I stared back at him, as if he didn't affect me at all. Finally, he turned around and walked into the darkness outside the firelight. Once he was out of sight, I took a deep gulp of air and focused on calming my racing heart. What was that all about?

"Hey, you actually came," JJ said from behind me.

"I was invited," I said. "How come I haven't heard about this full moon thing until now? Is it always here at the compound?"

"No, the families take turns hosting. In order to be one of the homes on the list, you have to back up to the forest and not be inside the developments in town," he said.

"But the forest runs through town. Don't people notice?" I asked.

He was shaking his head at me before I'd even completed my question. "No. By the time we have to shift, most people are inside for the night. Plus, since the families have been around forever, the towns expect there to be wolves in the forest. It wouldn't surprise them to come upon one of us. They just wouldn't know the difference between us and a regular wolf."

"Are there regular wolves in our forest?" I asked. I'd never seen one, but since my birthday last summer, I hadn't really looked. Had I come upon one, I'd have expected it to be a shifter.

JJ smiled at me. "Not anymore."

The others from my lunch group arrived and we all stood together in a circle next to the fire. I felt safer being in the group. Not because they had suddenly taken me in as one of their own, but because I knew what to expect from them. The other small groups of males, I didn't.

My guys were quieter and calmer from what I could tell. One of the groups I watched from the side was loud and rowdy. They were currently tossing each other around in what looked like a group wrestling match. They were constantly tearing someone's or even their own shirts off. I inched a bit closer to Shawn, hoping his large frame would shield me a little. Another group was heavily debating the need for keeping our world secret verses using our gift as shifters to gain power and money. Nice.

As the darkness grew fuller and the moon began to rise, the mood and tone of the night shifted from fun and camaraderie to something darker. My instincts were telling me maybe coming to the full moon party hadn't been such a good idea. Maybe I should go inside and leave it to the boys. Then there was the pride part of me that said I was being a baby. I'd fought for a spot in the clan, and I wasn't going to give it up just because I was feeling a little squeamish about all the hormone raging boys.

"You know, in my day, we were all one group," my grandfather said as he stepped into our little circle. "Now, there are so many of us that we have branched off into sects. It's nice to see so many of our ranks joining together."

I gazed around us and tried to see the men as he did. All I saw was trouble waiting to happen.

"It's just about time," he said. "Wouldn't you think?"

I wasn't certain who he was actually addressing. The boys were all nodding their heads back at him in agreement, though.

He yelled across the clearing, "It's almost time. Take in the small ones."

He was right, though. Almost as soon as the words left his mouth, boys and men started changing while the younger non-shifter boys were hustled out of the clearing toward the house. Where would they go for the night? Who would care for them?

The change wasn't usual or normal. When we wanted to shift, we simply pushed the shift forward and changed. It wasn't slow and tedious or even painful. Aside from the first time I'd shifted, it wasn't scary either.

The shifting that was taking place now was different. The men were fighting it. I could see by the anger in their eyes and the difficulty in the change. JJ dropped to his knees and howled. I couldn't tell if it was in rage or pain, but the sound echoed around me and raised the hair on the back of my neck.

I took a step back, suddenly uncertain of myself. I was the only one not being forced to shift. Everyone else who could shift did, even the old men. Clothes were left in piles of rags on the trampled grass.

I watched in horror by the firelight as what should have been fast and painless, was slow, agonizingly slow, and appeared painful. I bent down to JJ and looked into his eyes and saw that I was right. He was in pain. Why? I didn't know what to do or how to help. I grabbed his still shifting shoulders and screamed at him, "Stop fighting it. You're making it worse."

He growled in warning then snapped his shifting jaws and teeth at me, just missing my face.

"JJ! Please, don't fight. Just shift over," I said, pleading with him to listen, to try.

He didn't or he couldn't. Instead, he dropped all the way to the ground and howled at the moon. All around me, the males were making that sound. I covered my ears and turned in a circle, trying to find a place that wasn't full of writhing, half-naked men.

Then, silence eerily descended upon the clearing. I stood alone in the mass of full, strong wolves. I felt myself begin to perspire and fear skittered down my back. I needed to shift, and I needed to shift quickly. I took one step backward, and then another as I tried to keep my eyes on the mass of males that appeared to be keeping an eye on me.

Then, as if by unspoken command, the group as one dove forward. I didn't know what their intention was, but I wasn't going to find out. My plan had been to find a spot of privacy and change discreetly. That didn't happen. I shifted on the run. I turned and in one motion, pulled the wolf forward in my mind with a furious and panic-induced motion. It didn't matter, though, as my shift was easy and fluid. There wasn't pain, and there wasn't even real awareness of the changing. It was one motion from human to wolf and there I was – full-bodied she-wolf, powerful in my own right. I wasn't afraid of the males in that form. I was strong and able. Had I been in human form, I'd have laughed and screamed my joy. As the wolf, I threw my head back and howled for all I was worth to the night. The males, I didn't know if it was all of them or some, but a huge force howled right behind me.

What had felt menacing in human form was playful and silly as a wolf. We ran in packs, silently racing the night across the sky as well as one another. It was fun and it was joyous. The run was primal and we were fierce within the night.

We ran and ran for hours. We circled the town and we ran along the edges of the forest. We taunted the world of humans to come out and see us or to listen and hear us. We howled and we growled and we barked throughout our night. That's what the full moon was – it was ours.

Finally, as the sun began to crest over the far horizon, we slowed. I ran until I came to a section of pine trees I knew and loved. I hadn't planned on making that my bed for the night, but when it was time, I knew that was the place I wanted to be. I raced there and was glad to see it when it came full into view. I circled around to the biggest tree and happily laid down on the soft, thick bedding of pine needles that covered the forest floor.

I rolled around on my back and when I was content with my spot, I flopped over on my side, ready to rest. A group of wolves hesitated just outside my little pine haven. I had my suspicions as to who they were. The only one I knew for certain was Derek. The black wolf had shadowed me all night. Was it protection because he cared or was it protection because he thought I was his property? The others I believed and hoped were my lunch mates. Maybe they liked me, just a little. Regardless, I chuffed a breath at them all and welcomed them into my small spot.

They circled around and took up spots around me. In the end, after all was said and done, I was enclosed safely within a circle of male wolves. As a human I smiled. As a wolf, I closed my eyes and allowed sleep to claim me.

I awoke several hours later still within my protective circle of guys. The only problem was that I was the only one who had held the wolf. The others had shifted back to human form while they slept, naked human form.

I wasn't sure what to do about that. Did I pretend to sleep to allow them some dignity or did I just pretend it was no big deal? Neither. On silent feet, I slipped outside the circle and headed home.

I slept most of the day away, which I believe most of the wolves did because no one bothered me.

Chapter Six

Monday came around and with it, another first day of school. It was my first day at the Slate Center of Academics. I wasn't all that nervous. Well, maybe a little, as firsts always make me nervous, but not like the week before. One reason was that I hoped to know some of them. I hadn't seen any of the other clan in weeks and weeks, not since the night of the gathering where I joined with my wolf and in the process stopped a huge battle that never should have even gotten to that point.

I dressed in my comfy jeans and a yellow t-shirt. I glanced in the mirror to see how much I'd changed in the past weeks. The short answer was not much. My hair was a little bit lighter, thanks to the sunshine, but otherwise it was still brownish blondish. It was a little longer, still wavy, as usual. It was a bit of a wild mess. Not tangled and gross, but untamed. I loved it. A bit of wild in my life was a good thing. I looked liked me.

I grabbed a pair of flip-flops to complete my outfit and carried them down to the kitchen with my bag.

No one was around; however, fresh bagels and fruit were laid out for me. I grabbed a bagel and water from the fridge and went in search of Alex. He wasn't hard to find, being just outside the door with the car. I waved at him with my bagel and got in on my own. We were off to school without a word. I didn't like having a chauffeur. It seemed like it would be nice, but, yeah, not so much for me. Maybe the first day was kind of new and exciting, but on a daily basis, no, it wasn't.

We arrived and I got my first look at the Slate Center. I laughed. For two clans who acted like they were so different and so individual they sure did a lot of things the same. The Slate Center was almost exactly the same as the Griffin Academic Center. I mean, down to the brick, the entryway, the color, and the sidewalk, it was the same. The only reason I knew Alex had taken me to the right place was the big bold capital letters on the brick beside the door emblazed with the name.

I'd sat in the car long enough for Alex to get out and get to the door. Darn it. I got out and thanked him, even though he knew I didn't really care for the help. He still did it whenever given the chance. It bugged me.

I didn't even make it to the door before I was scooped up off my feet and enclosed in a bear hug to beat all bear hugs. "Boy, are you a sight for sore eyes!" Max said.

"Oh, my God!" I said once I was set down and able to get a look at him. His dark hair was shaggy and long. It almost covered his blue eyes. "You need a haircut!" I said and hugged him tight once more. Max was a friend from my time spent with the Slate men upon my first few weeks of shifting. He'd been one of the few that hadn't liked me just because I was a girl shifter but because he simply liked me, Abby.

"God, I'm so glad to see you! What have you been up too! Wow, you look great!" I was all excited and so relieved to know I would not be alone and an outcast here. "Who else will be here? Where is William?"

"Whoa, slow down, little one," he said. "William had to go back to school. Taylor headed off with him this year. He left about two weeks back. Charlie, Oscar, and Dillon will be here with us, though."

"He didn't say goodbye." Max thankfully didn't pretend he didn't know that I was talking about William. Even though we had left things a little strained between us, I'd thought we were still friends. I thought he would have told me if he was leaving. Called me, texted me, something. Instead, I'd heard nothing from him since the night I joined with my wolf and found balance. The same night I'd told him I wasn't choosing him over my family. The same night I moved in with my grandfather. It was only a few weeks ago, but it felt a lot longer.

"He isn't far away, you know," he said, slinging an arm around my shoulders. "Plus he will be back next full moon."

"No, I didn't know. Why will he be back?"

"Everyone comes home for the full moon. We need a place to run and be safe when we're forced into the change."

"Full moon parties," I said.

"Exactly. Didn't see you over the weekend, though. Where did you spend the change?" he asked.

"The event was at my grandfather's house this time. You know that's where I'm living right?" I asked him. I hadn't seen anyone and wondered if maybe they didn't know where to find me.

"We knew," he said.

I wanted to ask why they hadn't contacted me but decided maybe I didn't want to know. I was in too good a mood to let it be ruined by getting my feelings hurt. "Oh, well then, where did you guys spend the full moon?" I asked.

"At one of the cousins," he said. "How did it go?"

I shrugged. "It was fine. Since I am not forced into the change like the rest, it was a little strange to be in the middle."

"You don't change?" he asked. "But everyone changes during the full moon. Everyone."

"Nope. I'm special, remember?" I said. "Hey, that reminds me. Can I ask you something about the full moon?"

"Yeah, I know you're special, but...sure ask away. I'll answer if I can," he said.

"Shifting to wolf isn't painful. It never has been for me. I know it looks painful and it should be with all the popping and shifting bones and teeth and all that, but it's not. Is it the same for you and most of the males?"

"Usually," he said. "I mean, when we want to change, it is. It's fast, quick, and almost over before you think about it, right?"

"Yeah, it's the same for me, but when the change came over everyone on Saturday, it seemed different, painful."

"Well, sort of, I guess," he said. "It's a mental thing with some of us. I just accept that I am going to change when the moon rises. I know it's coming and I don't fight it. I don't take it personal and I don't get mad and focus on the fact that I am being forced to do something against my will. So it doesn't hurt me. But..." he said and looked around as if worried someone would hear him talking to me, as if it were some big secret. "Some of the others fight the change. They feel like they are being forced to do something against their will, so they fight the change and they stay aware during it, which means they feel every shifting muscle, every hair push through their skin, every growth of the spine to the tail. They feel it all, and it's painful."

"But why?" I asked. "Why do they fight it? They know it's going to happen. They can't stop it."

He shrugged and said, "You did. You weren't forced into a shift."

"That's different. I'm different," I said.

"So. They want it to be possible, and they want control back over their bodies. They fight it. I would say the more people who realize you aren't forced into a change every full moon, the more they will begin fighting it as well because if you can do it, why can't they?"

"Well, they could do it. You could do it too you know. You all need to embrace your wolves. Once you do that, it's a wide-open world out there," I said.

He shook his head, but smiled all the same and said, "Come on. Let's get to class. I don't want to get into your 'finding balance' discussion right now."

"Whatever. You know I'm right," I said smugly as I walked with him to class. "Let me guess, my schedule for Slate will be the same as it was at Griffin?"

"Yep," he said as we rounded a corner and entered a replica of my classroom at the other school.

"This is just too weird." I sat down in a seat that matched the one I'd been assigned the week before at the other school.

Max stopped me though and said, "Why are you sitting back there? Come on, sit with us."

Us being Charlie, Dillon, and Oscar. They were more of my Slate friends from the summer with William. They were sitting in a little clump closer to the front of the room. They held open a spot for me within their group. "You guys," I said getting a bit misty at the welcome.

Oscar and Dillon, the twins, were the same as always, with their brown hair and dark eyes, smiling from ear to ear. They each stood and gave me a hug. "It's about time you came over to the good school. Slumming it at the GAC last week?" Dillon asked.

I swung out a playful hand at Dillon and said, "Maybe I'm slumming it this week. I'll let you know what I think this afternoon."

Charlie was darker in coloring than the others, and he was just as happy to see me. He wrapped his arms around my middle and hugged me so tightly that I was lifted up off the ground. "Where have you been, beautiful?" he asked.

I was so grateful for my little group of friends in the clan. Even though time had passed and I hadn't heard from them in forever, they welcomed me with open arms. "You guys really are the best."

"We know," Oscar said.

Class began when the teacher came in. I should not have been surprised, but I was absolutely shocked when Mrs. Smith walked in and took her place at the head of the class. She winked at me and said, "Okay, so where were you last week, guys?"

I leaned over and whispered to Max, "What is she doing here?"

"She's our Monday and Wednesday teacher," he said.

"Yeah, well, she's also my Tuesday and Thursday teacher on my off weeks," I whispered. "You clans make me crazy with all your keep-it-separate-but-same crap. You do know it would be a lot easier if you just had one school and one set of teachers, right?" Then a horrible thought hit me. "Oh, God. Please tell me Mr. Staton is not a teacher here. The Glen one."

"Um…" he said.

"You have got to be kidding me!" I shrieked.

"Abby? Is there something you wanted to say?" Ms. Smith asked, drawing the attention of the entire class to me.

I smiled, a big, wide, very uncomfortable smile, and said, "No. Sorry. I'm good."

Max smiled back and tried to restrain his humor. "He's our Friday guy."

"Lord," I said.

I sat back and enjoyed the nice day with Ms. Smith. I didn't want to know right then who the Tuesday/Thursday teacher was at the Slate School. I'd find out soon enough.

Lunch arrived and with it – salad. A great, glorious, full-veggie salad. "I love you guys," I said to the lunch crew. The same crew from the other school, by the way. Apparently, they worked in shifts in order to cover the flow. "You are welcome, dear," one replied. To Dillon, who was towering over me from behind me in line, I asked, "Why do they have the same teachers and crews? Are the office people the same as well?"

"We are a small community. The fewer non-shifters we let in, the safer we are."

That made sense. It was still weird.

I sat down with all my Grey boys. It was a bit crowded with everyone at the table, but I was so happy to be surrounded by friends and people that liked me. The noise was wonderful. The conversation flowing around me was convoluted and loud and music to my ears. The silence of the last week had worn on me more than I realized. How was I going to go back to it the next week, having found such joy for the first time in what felt like forever?

Soon, other tables of people I didn't know were sliding chairs in to join us. Tables were scooted over to make more room. I was enfolded within them like I had always belonged.

The end of the day came, and honestly, I was sad. Not that I was all that enamored with school in general but because of all the people and how they took me in. It was a great day, and I had hopes for a great week.

I sat in the car with the usual cold formalities.

"Thank you, Alex."

"You are welcome, Miss."

There was one small change to the program, though. "We have one stop to make before heading back to the house," Alex said.

"Okay? What?"

"Your father has requested a moment of your time," he said.

"Great," I said, but with a quiet sarcasm I wasn't certain he heard as there was no further reply from him until we reached my former home.

I hesitated at the door again, which made me instantly annoyed. I slammed open the door and stomped in. My good mood of the day vanished in that instant. My father stayed sitting in the living room at my entrance, but he did acknowledge me. "Good afternoon. How was your day at the Slate school?"

"Fine," I said.

"How was everyone over there?"

"Fine," I said again. What was he after?

"That's all you have to say? Fine?"

It didn't matter what the conversation was between my father and me, it always ended up with me feeling defensive and him getting mad. There was no reason to expect otherwise, so I replied, "When I am taking part in the return of the Spanish Inquisition, yes. It was fine. Nothing of note happened today. I had all the regulated classes and even the same teacher as I did at the other school. What is it you would like me to say?"

He sighed and stood up. He was a tall man. Well-built and heavily muscled. In fact, he appeared thicker and stronger than he had a few months back. Apparently, living with my mother did him good. "I simply thought we could have a conversation. Your mother wanted to see you. She is feeling better today."

I felt a slight twinge of guilt because I hadn't thought of her in days even though I knew she was not doing well with her pregnancy. Part of it was intentional. I didn't want to know about the baby, so if I didn't think about them, then it wasn't really happening. It was a small mind game, but it was all I had.

"Oh. Where is she?" I asked.

"She's out back, getting some fresh air," he said. A small half smile appeared for just an instant on his face. It vanished almost as quickly. I felt my heart stutter a little at the slight show of emotion. He wasn't allowed to be soft and sweet about my mother. He was supposed to be a controlling jerk all the time, not just with me.

"Fine." I turned on my heels and headed out back. I wasn't sure what to say to her. I wasn't sure I even wanted to. I was still mad at her.

I stepped out the door and was annoyed at myself for the joy I felt at seeing my mother. Why couldn't I shut that down? Why did I have to still love her when she didn't seem to love me back anymore? Maybe in a small way she did, but it was all different since he'd showed up.

She looked tired and pale. Her hair was dry and dull, not the shiny locks it used to be. She turned when she heard my footsteps and I saw that even though she looked a bit worse for wear, she looked happy. Her eyes skipped right over me and moved to where my father stood behind me. An almost crushing pain clamped over my heart. I was nothing to them. Why was I even there? Why had she asked to see me? She didn't give a crap about me one way or another. It was all about him now.

"How are you, honey," my father asked her as he bent over to place a very sweet and gentle kiss on her lips. It made me sick. Not because it was a kiss, but because that was not who he was. How could he be so sweet with her and such a complete jerk to me all the time?

I felt my wolf get jumpy inside my skin. I listened to my heartbeat to try to calm down. I had counted to almost twenty by the time my mother actually looked my way.

"Abby, dear," she said as she held out her hand to me. I looked at it, then back up to her face. I didn't make a move to take hold of her hand. She wasn't old. She wasn't an invalid. Why was she acting so odd? Finally, she let her hand fall back to her lap, but her face, once happy with the attention given by my father, fell at the sight of me and my refusal of physical contact. What did she expect?

I wasn't going to drop down at her feet and thank her for their exalted presence. I was thinking of all kinds of sarcastic, mean thoughts that I was too scared to say out loud. Regardless of our relationship at that moment, I still respected her as my mother. I hated that I did, but sixteen years was hard to erase in a matter of weeks.

"Mother," I said by way of response, "I have been ordered to your side. Here I am."

I tried to come off as bored, but the tone had been off and instead I came across as petulant. I'd have to work on that, apparently.

She stuttered over herself a moment but then said, "I wanted to see how you were. How was your first day of school?"

"Which one, Mother? The real first day of the new school year was a week ago. Why do you care now?"

"Oh, but I thought today was your…oh. I'm so confused lately. I can't seem to keep things straight in my head. I'm sorry," she said.

"It's fine, dear. She's just being childish," my father said.

I didn't think I was the childish one, but then again, what did I know? I was just their unwanted, cast away child.

"Yes, dear," I said, heavy with the sarcasm. "It's fine that you forgot me. Besides, you have your real child to worry about. Don't worry about this one. I'm sure I can be erased from your thoughts as easily as you guys erased me from your house."

"Abby," my mother said. Her voice was hurt, but what came through clear and loud was her anger.

My father's voice joined in with, "Don't talk to your mother that way. You will show respect."

I had already turned to go, but I stopped and looked at them both and said, "Or what? You'll throw me out? Forget about me? Start a new life, a fresh start, without me? Oh, wait. You already did that. What more can you possibly do?"

Silence greeted my words. "That's what I thought," I said before I left them in the backyard.

I made it out the front door and halfway down the driveway before Brian stopped me. "Brian, I don't have time today. I'll have to catch up with you later," I said, trying to step around him.

He grabbed my arm, hard, and stopped me in my tracks. It took every ounce of self-control not to phase to wolf and tear him apart.

"Wait," he said. "I need to say something."

"What?" I said through my teeth. They were clenched so tightly that I was surprised I wasn't cracking them to bits as I held on to my temper.

He leaned in and whispered in my ear, "I know about your father and the others."

I didn't let my surprise and sudden trepidation show outwardly, but on the inside I was queasy with unease. "What about them?"

"I know what they are," he said.

"What are you talking about?" I snapped. I was going for exasperated. I think I pulled it off pretty well. "What are they?"

The hand around my arm grew increasingly tighter and painful as I realized Brian was angry. I'd never really seen him like that. His face grew red and tight little lines around his mouth appeared. "Don't play with me, Abby," he said up close to my face now.

I was suddenly very afraid. Partly by what he said and partly by what he didn't. Regardless, fear jumped around inside me without restraint. "I…I'm not."

"The demon wolves!" he screamed in my face. A small fleck of saliva flew from his lips and I felt it land squarely on my cheek, just under my eye. I tried to step back from his fiery anger, but he held me too tightly. I could have fought him, but I didn't want to show any real strength in the face of what he had just said.

I looked around to see if there were any of the demon wolves in sight that could come and help me out, but for once, there were not. Figured that the one time I actually needed their assistance they were nowhere to be found. Maybe that was a good thing. I had no idea what they would do. Going wolf would not be a good thing right then for any of us.

"Brian, I told you several weeks ago that we got a dog," I said calmly and softly. I didn't know if my tone would help the tense moment or not, but I was going to try anything I could to calm the situation down without resorting to proving, accidentally or on purpose, anything about the wolves or my family or me. "You met him, I think, right?"

His eyes bore into mine. He was breathing fast and hot against my face. Then, out of nowhere, I saw him relax. The muscles in his neck that had been standing out and fierce a moment before were lax and normal. His eyes, once wide and stark, softened. He came back to the real world before my eyes, and the mania settled back to confusion. He stepped back out of my space and lowered his eyes to the ground. Without really talking to me, he said, "Maybe you don't know then. Maybe you aren't one of them. They said there weren't any girls."

"They? They who? What are you talking about, Brian? What is going on?" I asked.

He let go of my arm and said, "I need to go." Then he turned around and left me standing in the driveway alone. I rubbed my arm where he'd held onto me and replayed what he had said.

"Miss Abigail?" Alex asked. He stood in the open door of the car, but his eyes were on the retreating back of Brian. "Are you all right?"

I turned back to see Brian disappear around his house and out of sight. Was I all right? "Yeah," I said and quickly got into the car. "I'm ready to go home."

"Yes, Miss," Alex said.

It was another quiet ride. I wasn't in the mood for conversation anyway. One thought kept circling around in my mind. Who was 'they?'

Chapter Seven

"How was your visit with your mother?" my grandfather asked the moment I walked in the door. It left me with the feeling that he already knew the answer. Had my father called and told on me?

I wasn't in the mood for games, so I said, "Not so great, actually."

He lifted one white eyebrow and said, "Oh?" As if he didn't already know. When I didn't say anything back, he pressed forward and asked, "Why do you think that is?"

"Because they hate me," I said bluntly.

"You and I both know that is not the case," he said.

"No, we both don't," I replied hotly.

"They would not call me every day to see how you are doing," he said.

I hadn't known they did that.

"And they wouldn't constantly make up reasons to get you to stop over just so they can see you," he continued.

"They do not," I replied, but there was a little spot of doubt shadowing my words. Maybe a little bit of hope too, which kind of ticked me off. I'd get that hope batted back down out of my heart and there it was, popping back up at the first hint of being wanted.

"Think it over, Abigail. Don't be so quick to judge them. They are having a hard time with everything too," he said.

"I doubt it," I replied. I crossed my arms over my chest in order to not fidget around. I didn't want him to see how much I wanted to believe him.

"You might want to remember – you left them. They didn't leave you," he said.

"I didn't leave them. They were shoving me out the door before I even thought about moving in with you. They were happy to get rid of me. They already have a nursery going up in my room! If I hadn't moved out of there, I'd be out in a tent in the backyard by now."

"Abigail," he tried to interrupt, but I talked right over him.

"I may have been the one to leave first, but they were happy about it," I said, and I believed that much. If nothing else, that I knew was true. Maybe some small part of them did miss me or miss the idea of me, but they were happy with the living arrangements, whether they wanted to say it out loud or not.

We stared at one another for a long moment. Neither of us was willing to concede to the other right then. It wasn't an angry moment, but it was fueled by emotion all the same.

~ * ~

The next day arrived and with it came a bad case of lethargy on my part. I was down, feeling gray and sad. I dressed to fit my mood in black jeans, a black shirt, and black flip-flops. I pulled my hair up in a messy bun and didn't even bother with makeup before heading down for breakfast.

I wasn't in the mood and not happy to see my grandfather waiting for me in the kitchen. "I thought I would see you off this morning," he said, trying a smile out on me. It was stiff but a smile all the same. Weird.

Before I could come up with a response to his greeting, he surprised me by tossing his nose up in the air and drawing in a long, deep breath. What the heck? He stood quickly and stalked to where I stood, all the while taking deep breaths through his nose. I tried to take a step back, but he reached out and took hold of my elbow to stop me. It wasn't a harsh hold, but it held me in place all the same.

He leaned in toward my neck and sniffed. Normally, this would have flipped me out, but he was so intent on what he was doing, it was freaking me out in a different way. "What is it?" I asked him, afraid to find out but needing to know.

He jerked upright and stepped away from me. He turned and looked out the window that looked out over the backyard to the forest.

"Grandfather?"

"I think you need to meet someone," he said cryptically.

"Okay. Who?"

He didn't turn around. He kept his back to me with his hands clasped behind him. "Come straight home after school today. I'll talk to you about it then."

"But,"

"No," he barked. "After school, we will talk."

I slipped the strap of my bag over my shoulder and left without another word.

My day didn't get better. Alex, normally very stoic and distant, hovered over me at the door that morning. He was close to the point of making me uneasy. "Alex?" I asked as I pulled away from him. He was so close I could see the small lines around his mouth.

"Can I help you with anything, Miss?" he asked but didn't move away even a fraction of an inch.

"No," I said, but it sounded like a question. I didn't understand what was going on. He stayed there. Staring. It wasn't until my grandfather stepped outside and snapped at him that he finally closed my door. He quickly got in the car and we were off to school. He didn't get out to get my door once we arrived. He stayed up front – door closed, window up. What the heck?

Things got weirder at school. The moment I stepped out of the car, all the boys within a few feet of me, and I mean *all the boys*, flocked around me like a dog to sheep, or fish to water, or girls to chocolate. Didn't matter what you called me, they were on me like Velcro from the moment I stepped onto the walkway.

"Morning," I said and picked up my pace to get inside. No one answered, but they stayed close and in my personal space. I was very nervous. Something was so wrong. I didn't know what, though.

I immediately headed to my classroom and tried to find safety within my little group of guys, but while I usually felt protected by them, they were possessive and even a bit handsy, which set me off.

"Good morning, Abby," Max said.

Those words should not have halted me in my steps. They were just your normal, everyday words, right? They were said slow and drawn out, though. His blue eyes, which normally were sparkly and happy, were squinty and direct on my form. Not on me, my face, but from my feet to the top of my head he stared. Up and down his eyes traveled my body and my heart dropped into my stomach. Yes, something was very wrong.

He approached me and I thought it was to give me the customary hug he always seemed to bestow, but instead of a safe hug, his hands dropped down and patted my rear. I jerked back and pushed him away. "Hey. Hands off!" I didn't yell, but the tone was just as strong.

Max backed up. He shook his head once, but then I saw his eyes unfocus. What the hell was that?

Dillon and Oscar boxed me in as I was watching Max. "Yeah, good morning," Dillon said. Oscar stayed quiet, but his eyes were harsh and weighed heavily on me. I tried to back up. I tried to give myself some room from my friends. I backed up into a hard body. Heat was emanating from it in waves. I spun around and faced Charlie. His eyes.

My wolf was quiet but at attention within me. She wasn't clamoring to be set free, but she was preparing for something, though. I could feel the intensity of her concentration.

Then, when for the second time in less than a minute I felt someone place a warm possessive hand on my left butt cheek, I flipped out. I don't know why I let it happen, but suddenly I felt the wolf in me attack from within. I phased over and let my wolf take over. I snapped my teeth down hard on the offending hand and held. I would teach the groper a little lesson in manners and keeping their hands to themselves. I clamped tighter when he tried to pull free. I felt the skin under my teeth give way and my mouth suddenly filled with blood.

My vision clouded over with red and my ears held only the noise of a high-pitched whine of sound. No other sights or sounds made it through to my mind. My muzzle was jerked left then right, but I held tight to the hand and even clamped down further until my teeth hit something hard. Was it bone? Was it cartilage? I didn't care. I swallowed the salty liquid that hit my tongue and licked the hand for more.

I began to hear my heartbeat along with the squeal of sound fogging my head. I knew something was wrong with me, but I couldn't get past the need and desperate desire for the liquid gold I had in my mouth. The human me was screaming for attention. The wolf was happy and in control. Neither was in control, though.

A heavy weight dropped down onto my back. My legs shook under the impact, and unable to bare it, I dropped flat to the ground to my belly. I lost hold of the hand. I felt it tear its way out of my teeth as I was pushed to the floor. I was devastated at its loss.

My head was shoved down forcefully by many hands to the floor and held there. I began to struggle under the restraint. I tried to wiggle and writhe away, but there were too many of them holding me down. I tried to focus in on their faces, but everything was still filled with red. I snapped at one pair of hands. I growled and snarled. I couldn't hear the sound, but I felt the rumbling through my body.

A flash of lightning hit behind my eyes, and everything went dark and still.

~ * ~

I forced my eyes open. They felt so heavy that it took more energy than I expected. When I finally pried them open, the world before me was blurry and way too bright. I squinted and let my eyes adjust for a moment. Then I tried to take in my surroundings.

A warm, comforting weight was on my head. It took me a second to figure out it was a hand, resting between my ears and buried in fur. That left me with additional questions. Why was I in wolf form, and who's hand was that?

I lifted my head and saw Derek sitting next to me. He was sprawled out in a red chair, and his eyes were directly on mine.

He didn't remove his hand; in fact, he scratch behind one of my ears and then left his hand where it was. Why did that always feel so nice? "You all right now, little beast?" he asked softly.

I was still playing catch up in my head, trying to figure out what happened. Was I all right? I'd been going to class when I'd felt threatened by the crowd of boys, and then…oh. I remembered. I'd shifted and attacked someone. Then I'd been overpowered by them all and knocked out. Whose hand had I torn apart? Was he okay? Ow. Was that why my head ached horribly? What had they hit me with?

"Are you going to shift back so we can talk?"

What was Derek doing there, at the Slate school of all places? He was the wrong clan type to be there.

As if reading my mind he said, "The school called your grandfather, who called your dad, who then asked me to come get you."

I didn't question why Derek and not my family, as it was probably a smart move on their part. I didn't think my grandfather or my father would have been all that calm in the Slate school, especially after what had happened.

"Honey, we need to talk," he said.

Honey? I sat up. His hand drifted off my head, and I was bereft of the comfort for some reason. The small amount of contact made me feel less alone. With it gone, I was again isolated. Separate. Different. I shook off the melancholy and hopped down to the floor from the little cushioned couch I had been laying on.

The muscles in my back and neck around my shoulders were rough and sore. Not to the point of painful, but noticeably uncomfortable. I stopped in front of the door and waited for Derek to get the hint that I was ready to get out of there.

He leaned over with his arms on his knees and again made contact with my eyes. "We need to talk first, Abby."

I whined at him. It was a sad, dejected sound, and it said more than words would have. I didn't want to talk. I wanted to leave. I needed to get out of there and go home and figure out what the hell had happened. Why had my friends turned on me? What was wrong with everyone lately?

He stood and came over to me. With both hands he lifted my face up to his and looked deeply into my eyes. He was so close his nose was pressed against my moist wolf one. I was nervous with his nearness, but for some reason I didn't want him to stop. Maybe it wasn't just everyone else that was weird. Maybe I was weird too. Something was off.

"All right. I'll take you home, but we have to talk."

He was right. He and my grandfather too, probably, would want to know what happened. The problem was, I didn't know either.

He opened the door and stalked out of the room. I hesitated in the doorway. I was afraid to go out. Would they attack me again? I looked left and right. I didn't see anyone. Derek stopped at the exit doors and waited for me. I took one last look around to make sure I was safe and ran to him. I pressed up against his legs. It made me feel safer to be close to him. He'd come and stayed with me while I was unconscious. I didn't know why, but for that, I would trust him for the moment, no one else.

He again put his hand on my head and I felt better. Just that one touch and I was steady.

"You are safe, little beast. I won't let anyone hurt you," he said quietly for my ears only.

He opened the door to the car. Alex hadn't gotten out to do it. I hesitated, remembering how strangely he'd acted that morning. Just like everyone else had. I didn't want to get in. I whimpered my concern.

Derek glanced down then toward Alex. His back was to us, as he sat in the driver's seat of the car. He didn't turn to look at us. He didn't even glance in the rearview mirror.

"Come on," he said. "You're good."

I glanced back again and wondered how far from home was I? Could I run it? I was just thinking that I could when Derek broke into my thoughts and said, "Don't even think about it."

Yep, there was the controlling Derek I knew and didn't love. If I had been in human form, I'd have smiled just for the shear normalcy of him. I got into the car. Not because I suddenly trusted everyone again, but simply because Derek was too stubborn to let anything go wrong in his presence.

72

I sat up on the seat and pressed my face to the window. I used my paw on the window button and slid it down enough to get my face out into the air. Something about being a wolf made me unhappy being cooped up inside a car. The window being down helped.

We arrived home without incident, and Derek walked with me inside. I expected him to leave, but he didn't. Then when I entered one of the family rooms, I realized why. My grandfather was there, along with my father.

"I got her. She's all right. A little worse for wear, and not ready to shift back, but all in all, she's good," Derek said, plopping himself down in one of the cushy chairs by the windows.

Those chairs were a set of two, and they happened to be my favorite chairs as well, but I didn't think I would be allowed up on them in my current form, so instead I sat down in front of the unlit fireplace and waited to see what would happen next. I was a bit surprised to see a family meeting. I couldn't remember my father stepping foot in the house since I moved in.

"We waited too long," my grandfather said.

"I didn't even know it was an issue," my father replied. "You should have told us."

Told us what? Waited to long? What was going on?

My grandfather growled him into silence then said, "We haven't had it come up in about fifty years at this point. I forgot until this very morning, when I scented her."

I growled at them all with his words. Why was everyone always worrying about how I smelled? My God, I was not a tulip.

Derek stifled a choking laugh. He knew what I was thinking. They all did.

"Abigail, please go shift into your human form," my father demanded.

I dropped down to lay on the floor. I put my head on my front legs and closed my eyes with a huff. It was as effective a way of telling him no as I could think of. He got the message.

"Why do you have to fight me on every single thing!" he roared and stalked over to me to...to what? I will never know because Derek jumped to his feet and stepped between us. Another why swam through my mind.

My father stood chest to chest with Derek as his breath loudly heaved in and out. Derek, however, stood firm and solid, not breathing heavy at all. What was going on?

My grandfather answered my unspoken question. "Stop! Adam, you are being affected by her. You should leave. Actually, Derek, you should as well as apparently you are too, only in the protective manner instead of the aggressive that Adam is. I need to have a discussion with Abigail. Alone."

The more answers I received, the more confused I became. I wasn't doing anything. How could I be the problem?

My father glared at me, but then he turned and left without argument or another word. Nothing new there. Derek squatted down in front of me and ran his hand over my head and down my neck. I waited for him to say something, but he didn't. His face was closed of emotion, as usual. When he stood and left without another word, I wasn't surprised. Not really. Some other emotion, however, zinged me instead. Regret maybe?

I glanced at my grandfather. He looked tired. He slumped down onto the sofa and turned to look out the window. I needed to know what was going on, and apparently he was the one who could tell me. I brushed against his legs as I walked passed him then quickly rushed up the stairs where I shifted back to two legs. I dressed in some yoga pants and a tee and went back downstairs.

I sat down next to him. "Okay, I'm here. What's going on?"

He turned to me with intense eyes and through gritted teeth said, "Maybe you should sit over there." He pointed to the chair Derek had recently vacated.

I stood up, trying all the while not to allow my feelings to be hurt by his obvious aversion. I perched in the chair he indicated way across the room and waited. I tried to calm my sudden anger at the day and tried to settle my racing thoughts.

"I have contacted Lady Lilly."

"Who is Lady Lilly?" I asked.

"She is a woman of our kind, one of the last. She is expecting you to visit her tomorrow. She is very old and unable to shift anymore, but she was able to when she was in her prime. She married, had several children, all boys, and she has settled into her retirement very nicely. She lives a bit away from us, but I believe the journey will do you some good, as well as give you and the…young men some space."

There was only one shifting woman left? Where was she? How come she wasn't here with the rest of the clans?

"You don't want to discuss what happened today? Don't you care that I was mauled and beaten down by those young men you think I need to give a break too?" I asked. I was trying to remain respectful to him, but I was having a bit of a problem doing so.

"I know what happened," he said.

I was getting madder by the second. Why was everything so classified and secret? Just talk to me. Tell me what was going on. Then I realized the man was sweating. A lot. His face was moist and the hair around his temples was wet. "Grandfather? Are you okay?" If he had a heart attack, I wouldn't know what to do. Can a wolf shifter go to the hospital?

"You are emanating a smell or a hormone that is aggravating my wolf. I'm having a hard time keeping him under control. You should maybe go," he said. His teeth were clenched tightly.

Eww. This was my grandfather and I was enticing him? Gross! "I'll just go to my room then. I'll see you in the morning." I didn't care about the why at that moment. I just wanted to get out of there.

"I'll leave instructions for you," he said.

I had already left the room when I thought of something. I peeked my head around the doorframe and said, "Alex is not a good fit for the drive. He's acting funny around me too." I left him to figure out how to get me out to Lady Lilly's. He wanted me to go, fine. I'd go and meet her, but he could work out the semantics of it all.

I lay in bed that night thinking. Who was Lady Lilly? Why did she leave the family area? How far away was far? How old was she? I had a lot of questions. Maybe I needed to focus on the fact that I would finally have a girl to talk to about being a wolf. Someone that could understand how I was feeling. Someone that had gone through what I was. I was excited and nervous all at the same time. What if she didn't like me? What if I wasn't what she expected?

I wished I could call my mom. I needed someone to talk to, but there was no one left for me. Brian, I couldn't talk to because I was a shifter and he wasn't and he wasn't allowed to know I was a shifter. William was back at school and hadn't reached out to me in weeks. The Grey clan had attacked me, which pretty much took them out of my confidence circle. Derek, I didn't know what to think of him. One second he was an ass, and the next he was caring and compassionate. My father, yeah, that wasn't happening. He and I simply were not seeing the same side of things. I wasn't sure if we ever would. The one person I had always been close to, had always been able to share anything and everything with, was my mother, and she was no longer available at all to me. She'd changed. I'd changed. We would never be the same. I was more alone than I'd ever been before. I had no one and no one even wanted me.

There I was, the only shifting female left and no one wanted me. I was the only balanced wolf at all within the clans, and that still wasn't enough. What did I need to do to prove that I was worthwhile to someone? Not just because I was pretty or a shifter, but because I, Abigail Staton, was worthwhile.

I angrily swiped away the tears that were running down my cheeks. They were as worthless as I was. I didn't want to cry and feel sorry for myself. I did anyway. I buried my face in my pillow and cried myself to sleep. It wouldn't solve anything, but at that point, I didn't care.

Chapter Eight

I awoke the next morning feeling a bit worse for wear. My eyes showed the restless night along with the tears. I felt adrift for the day since I couldn't go to school. Actually, I didn't know for certain if I could not go to school, but after the events of the day before, maybe not going was better for everyone, at least until I could find out why.

I pulled on jeans and a plain tank top, grabbed a hoodie out of my closet, and called it good enough. As I stepped down the stairs, I smoothed my hair into a quick ponytail. I didn't care what it looked like, especially since my looks didn't matter to the wolves. All that seemed to be important was that I smelled.

Smelled like what, though? Was it a perfume type thing, all flowers and chemical, or was it skunky and musky, but something I could not smell. Whatever it was, I hated it. Ever since I became a shifter all I'd dealt with was people talking about my smell and I was sick of it. I was more than my scent.

I was smart. I was strong. I could shift like it was nobody's business. My hair was nice too, if I was going to be vain. It was long and multi-colored and thick as all get out. I personally thought I was a bit of a catch without all the smelling stuff.

In the kitchen, I found Peggy waiting for me. "Hey," I said. She was dressed in casual clothes like me, jeans and t-shirt. "What's going on?"

"It looks like I am your ride today," she said. "I made us some bagels to go. Whenever you are ready, we can head out. It should take us about two hours to get there even with a stop for gas and snacks."

"Is my grandfather coming too?" I asked. It wasn't that I was scared to go alone, but part of me was. I didn't know this Lilly chick. Having someone come along would make me feel better.

"No. He said he had things to take care of today that he couldn't reschedule," she said.

I should not have been surprised or hurt, but I was all the same. Something was always more important than I was to my family. I looked at Peggy. I hadn't had much contact with her during my stay at my grandfather's. I saw her around the house and she was nice and all, but we didn't really talk. "Okay. I guess I'm ready whenever you are."

"Let's go then," she said. She grabbed her purse that was sitting by the door and headed out. She didn't even look back to see if I was following. I sighed and trailed out after her. It was going to be a long trip.

Outside was a gray Toyota. Peggy unlocked the doors and we both stepped in. At least it wasn't a limo, right? I quickly fastened my seatbelt. I was feeling awkward and strange. I tried to think of a good conversation starter, but nothing came to mind. Thankfully, after she was on the road, Peggy turned on the radio loud enough to hinder discussion. I turned and watched out the window for a bit.

We didn't talk much, just stuff like, "Hey you ready to stop and find a soda and snack? We can go to the bathroom while we are there." That was about it, though. It was a long drive. As I said, she was always nice, but we didn't have much to say to each other.

We turned onto a dirt road and drove through a sparse pine forest. After a few miles, I saw a house come into view. It was big and white with tall windows and a wrap around porch. There were fall flowers in hanging pots all along the front. It was pretty. Not, in-your-face-money type, but big and welcoming. I loved it.

When I hopped out of the car, a pack of mutts came tearing around the house. They barked and growled and ran right at me. Their tails were wild and wiggly, high in the air behind them in greeting. I was not afraid of them at all. They weren't aggressive. They were friendly, full of life and joy. They stopped at my feet and then, as if all one creature, they jumped up on me and took turns trying to lick my face. I laughed and petted them and tried to get them down. "Stop, you silly dogs. Get down. Get down," I said through laughter.

"Boys! Off!"

I turned toward the firm voice and saw a beautiful woman. I don't mean she was pretty – she was absolutely lovely. The dogs dropped to the ground and ran to her. They were obviously obedient and loyal.

She wore a long white dress, cinched in at her tiny waist. She brushed her long, dark brown hair out of her face as she dropped down to a squat in front of her animals. She spoke softly to them as they sat prettily at her feet.

Then she stood and smiled in our direction. "Welcome to my home. I am so happy to meet you, finally!"

Peggy turned to me and said, "I'll just wait here."

"You aren't coming in with me?" I asked.

"No," she said and glanced again at Lady Lilly. "You're here to talk with her. Not me." She smiled and said, "Don't worry. I'll be fine. I have a book and time to myself. It will be a nice break for me. Really."

I still felt bad about her waiting outside in the car, but I didn't know how to remedy the situation, so I said, "I won't be too long."

She waved me off and said, "Take your time." I watched as she sat back down in the car, adjusted the seat back, and pulled out a book. She waved the book at me as if showing me she was good.

"You coming, honey?" Lilly asked from the porch.

"Yes." I walked over to meet her. Up close she was just as lovely as from afar. She was pushing what, seventy years old? Yet, she looked decades younger. Her dark brown eyes were big and clear and they were sharp and intense as they looked me over as I did her.

"It's about time you showed up. I don't mean today. I mean I have been waiting months to get the call that you were coming to visit," she said.

"I'm sorry. I didn't know about you until last night," I said. "No one tells me anything in this family."

She snorted and said, "It was the same way when I was your age. Those men..."

"Yeah," I said. "Not liking that all that much."

"Come on in out of the sun. I've made us tea. You drink tea, don't you?" she asked.

Not really. "Sure," I said.

We stepped inside and off to the right into a pretty little sitting room with a plush looking flowered couch in yellow. Two matching chairs sat in a bright circle of sunshine that filtered in through the windows. There was a white porcelain tea set waiting for us on a dainty little service cart. It was the type I'd seen in movies but never in person. The room was very girlie. There were watercolor paintings framed on the yellow walls. The sun came in and warmed the room through the sheer curtains at the windows that were pulled back with ties to match.

"This is a pretty room," I said, and I meant it. It made me feel...happy. Maybe it was the yellow, maybe it was the sun, but the room was comforting.

"This is my favorite room in the house. When my husband built this house, he told me that he'd made this room especially for me. I could decorate it any way I wanted, and I have, several times over the years."

"Where is your husband now?" I asked. Making small talk is not my biggest forte, but I was going to give it a go.

"He passed several years ago," she said.

I'd known that. My grandfather had told me, but with the nervousness of the meeting I'd forgotten. "Are you still sad over it?"

"He was my best friend before becoming my husband, and afterward we were inseparable. I have had my share of problems over the years, but having my husband at my side always made it bearable. Now that he is gone, I'm lonely. I miss him more each day."

"I'm very sorry," I said even though that seemed stupid. I didn't know the guy and I'd just met her. "What about your children? Do they live around here? Don't they come and see you?"

"Yes, but it's not the same thing," she said. "You'll find there is a difference between the love of children and friends and the love you have for your husband. I didn't know there was one until he was gone. No matter the company we keep, sometimes we still feel alone."

I knew the feeling very well lately. "How many children do you have?" I asked.

"Five," she said.

Five? Wow, that was a lot. I sat down on one of the dainty chairs next to the sofa and tried to think what to say next.

She took the worry away by cutting to the chase. "Well, I guess we better get chatting about being a girl and a wolf. I'm sure you have questions, so you may as well get asking. That's what I'm here for."

I laughed and said, "All right. I guess that makes sense. Why are all the males freaking out over me lately? My grandfather said I am putting off a hormone, but why now? Why not when I first changed?"

She handed me a perfectly poured cup of tea and said, "Men are such babies. They can't control themselves around a hamburger, let alone a lovely she-wolf that is going into heat."

"Heat?" I said mortified. I knew what that was in the animal kingdom, but I wasn't exactly an animal.

She sighed and said, "Yes. It really is that base of a thing. Human girls as you know have a period every month. Now that you are fully-grown into a shifter, some things are no longer human. Your reproductive cycle is one of those things. So, you will probably menstruate twice a year."

That was not what I was expecting, and I was feeling very awkward having the conversation of my period with a stranger. I mean really.

"However, what happens is about ten days to two weeks before you get your period, you become fertile."

"Oh, God," I said fearing what was coming.

"Yep. So your body is putting off a hormone due to being at your most fertile, and that is what is making all the boys crazy. They are a slave to their animals and can't or won't control themselves around you. Some will want to possess you. Some will want to control you. Some will not know what they want other than to protect you. All the boys will be aggressive. Some directly toward you as you are the cause of them being out of control. Some toward the other males in order to warn them off."

"But even the men in my own family are acting that way. That is so…"

"Yes. Icky. They will be the ones who are angry with you. They won't want to possess you, but they will be mad and aggressive all the same. It's your fault they are struggling to control their wolf. Doesn't matter that you can't do anything about it, it will still be your fault."

"So when I was attacked yesterday," I said.

"You will find, that even though it is not fair, and, no, it is not your fault, it may be easier to stay away from the boys during your heat period."

"How long is this heat?" I asked almost afraid to ask.

"Most animals are for a short period, maybe a week or ten days. We will last almost a full month,"

"A month!" I said, "What about school? How do I stay away from male wolves for a full month! I'm surrounded by them. They are everywhere."

She shrugged but said gently, "I know. It's very hard for girl shifters. At least the hard time is only about two weeks. There was only a handful of us when I was a girl. We banded together and made it through because we had each other. You don't have anyone else, except me, and you won't have me for much longer."

"Why? Are you going somewhere?" I asked.

"I'm sick," she said and shrugged again as if it was no big deal. "I'm old. It happens."

"But you don't look old," I said. "You look like my mom."

"That, my dear, is one of the perks of being a shifter female. We don't age like humans," she said.

I had a wild thought and decided to ask it even though it was a bit nosy, "Can you really not shift anymore?" She looked young and strong. It didn't make sense that she couldn't shift.

She smiled at me but didn't answer. Instead she said, "Some things, it's better to let people believe. I like being here in the home my husband built. Not being able to shift has allowed me to stay here. Otherwise I would have been forced back into the community after he died."

"So you lied."

"So I fibbed," she replied. "That is a difference you will understand when you are older and more experienced."

"Did you ever balance?" I asked.

"Not like you have, or so I have heard," she said. "What is it exactly? If you can explain."

I tried to think of a good way to explain it. "Well, before I came together, I felt like I was always trying to control the wolf inside of me. Then there was the wolf trying to take control away. We were in battle against each other all the time. You know what I mean?"

"Yes, I do. I fight my wolf for control all the time. She wants out to run and play and I don't want to. I don't want to change anymore. I don't want anyone to know I still can and make me come back to the community. I want to stay here."

"Why would you have to come back?" I asked. I mean she was an adult, an older adult. What could they possible want from her now?

"You are a girl in the community. How much control do they try to have over you," she said, a small half smile on her face.

"Yeah," I said, knowing exactly what she was saying. The men, they were a controlling bunch of brutes if you let them be. She was free out here. Yes, maybe she was lonely and sometimes alone, but I guessed that was better than being under someone else's rules and control. I can't imagine dealing with that at her age, regardless of how young she looked.

"Well, there came a moment when I stopped fighting the wolf and found a happy medium. She stopped fighting me. It was like magic. We came together like two halves and it was just…bam! There I was, no longer in a battle within my own body."

"So what does that really mean, though?" she asked. She was the first person to ask me anything about it, the first who actually wanted to know. I wondered if the others hadn't asked me because they were ashamed of not balancing before me. There I was, a newly shifting wolf, and I did it. Whereas they had been dealing with the wolves and the shifting since the beginning and they never had. Not one of them.

"It means that I can shift anytime I want to, and I'm not forced to change when I don't want to. I don't even have to change over during the first night of a full moon. I didn't know that was even a thing until last weekend."

"I always hate the full moon. I have to go into hiding during it. If anyone were to find out..."

"Yeah, after witnessing the effects of the moon and their attitude during it, I can see why it would not be a fun time. I hate being forced to do anything, but being forced into a change every month would be terrible. Did you ever get used to it?" I asked.

"No, I never did. It would be nice to not worry about it," she said.

"I can also partly shift. I wasn't like the rest of you long enough to know all that much about being two halves, but I can tell you that only shifting a hand into a claw without having to go into the full change is really nice sometimes. Effective in making a point."

She smiled and even breathed out a small laugh. "I can imagine. Especially with all those men."

"You got it."

"Do you think you could show me how to balance?" she asked.

"I wish I could," I said. I really did. Having someone else that had found that freedom would validate the effect of it to the others. I needed to try to help them, but until they were ready to listen, there wasn't anything I could do. "I think it's something each individual needs to figure out."

She didn't say anything for a long moment and I was afraid I had hurt her feelings. There she was trying to help me find my way through the world of wolves, all the while being a girl, and there I was not helping her. "I'm really sorry."

"It is what it is, dear," she said and took a sip of her tea.

I wracked my brain for an answer to the problem and finally said, "Maybe you have to stop fighting her," I said. "I mean your wolf. She is part of you and needs to be part of your life. Shutting her out keeps you out of balance. Maybe at the full moon next time, embrace her. Welcome her forward. See what that does."

"Hmm," was her only answer.

"I wish I could tell you more," I said. "Being balanced is great, but it doesn't help me out in the rest of my life, though."

"There is that," she said and smiled again. "You have found a balance with your wolf, but I have found a balance with my life. Maybe we both need a little work," she said.

"Yeah, I'm not doing so hot in that department."

"Can you explain why even the more docile, less aggressive Grey clan were the ones to attack me while the aggressive Staton side didn't? I would have expected it to be the other way around."

"All I can tell you is that the Greys like to pride themselves on their easy ways. The Statons aggressively control themselves all the time in all things. They will always have more control even though with it, they are a darker group of men, harder to take and harder to live with. The Grey's are all nice and easy going, but in reality, they are more out of control when in emotional situations. You need to remember, too, that most of them have never been around a female in heat. It would be a surprise. They wouldn't have ever had their wolves react so fiercely. They would not have expected to have to hold onto their animal instincts so tightly. Actually, I'm surprised it didn't end up worse than it did. I blame your father and grandfather for that. At least your grandfather should have known better. He's dealt with it. Your father should have a small memory of it at least. They should be ashamed of themselves for putting you at risk. Especially if they suspected you were coming into heat."

It dawned on me at that moment that she was right. They had to have known. The night before, they had known. I realized it right then. My father had been worse than usual, mean even. My grandfather had too. "Yes, they knew, and they let me walk into that school full of boys without preparing me, like a sheep in a lion's den. Why did they do that?"

She stayed still and sipped her tea. Carefully she set her cup on the table then she said, "That's a good question, one I can't answer. Maybe it's one you should ask."

"Not like they would answer me directly," I fumed. "How do you know my family? My grandfather?"

"He's my brother," she said.

"Oh, my God," I said. "Why didn't I know that? Why didn't anyone tell me I had a great aunt out there? Especially one that was like me!"

"Another good question for them," she said.

We talked for a long while. I told her of my life growing up with only my mother and how wonderful it was. How being just the two of us had made us so close. "That was why it was so hard when my father came home. I suddenly didn't matter at all. Everything revolved around him. I felt like an orphan. I got a father and lost my mother all in one moment."

"You can't be too hard on your mother. She's only human after all," Lady Lilly said.

"I don't understand what that has to do with anything."

"It's simple really. The part of us that makes us animals is also the part that draws humans toward us. Do they want to be around you now more than ever?"

"No," I said. "Not that I know of. Since I shifted, I haven't been around any humans, except for the ones that are part of the community already. They don't speak to me or want to be around me any more than anyone ever did. I'm just ordinary."

"Well, once you get out into the real world, you will find that humans will want to be near you. Will do anything for you. Would give up their souls to be with you. Which is why you can't be overly upset with your mother. She's human and can't help herself. Once she and your father are together for a while, it will wear off a little, but she will always choose him over you now that he is back in her life. She can't help it," she said.

"But that's kind of sick, don't you think?" I asked.

"What?" she said.

"Well, choosing humans to mate with when you know they are almost a prisoner to their own minds and hearts once you do. It's like possession. I want someone who wants to be with me because of me. Not because some juju power makes them," I said.

"High ideas from someone who has her pick of mates, don't you think?" she said. She wasn't mad, or I didn't think she was. She sipped her tea and watched me.

"What do you mean," I asked.

"Well, you are the first female born in two generations. What did you expect all those boys to do? Stay alone and single all their lives? Never have love? Never have children? You ask a lot of something you know nothing about, dear."

She was right. Had they not married regular humans, they would have been alone. Whereas I could have my pick of men. There were a lot my own age to choose from. "I'm sorry. You are right," I said. "It's not fair to ask them that."

She shrugged and said, "No worries, dear, a bit of advice, though. Don't go judging people for things you have not experienced yet. Until you have walked in their shoes or lived their lives or suffered their demons, don't judge. You may find they did what they had to do to get through. Don't be so harsh in life."

I felt my face heat in embarrassment.

She saw it too, and she chuckled and slapped a gentle hand on my arm and said, "Oh stop worrying so much. How are you supposed to learn things if no one ever tells you or teaches you? I will tell you anything I think you need to know and you should ask anything can think of. We girls need to stick together. There aren't many of us left."

It was afternoon by the time I stood to leave. I didn't want to go. I wished I could stay for a while – or forever. She was so much more than I expected and I wanted to soak up all her knowledge and all her life lessons. "I wish I could stay longer."

"I wish you could too. Some other time. You can come and spend a week or your month with me. We can plan for it," she said, wrapping her slender arms around me in a hug. "For your next heat, you can come here. It will be lovely."

"I am so glad I got to meet you. I'll come back soon. I promise," I said. One more thought crossed my mind before I left. "How do I get through the rest of this heat?"

"The first week is the hardest. Maybe stay away from everyone male for the next couple of days. It will reach a peak in a few days, and then you should get your period. By the third week, everyone will just act mad around you, and then cranky, and then everything will be back to normal for about six months."

"Okay. I guess I can get through this. It won't be as bad as I thought," I said. I gave her one last hug and walked out to the car. Peggy was chipper and happy and ready to get going.

"I'm sorry to have kept you so long. I didn't realize how much time had passes until I got hungry for lunch," I said.

"No problem. We can stop on the way back and get something to eat. Plus I need to use the facilities," she said.

"Why didn't you come in with me? I'm sure Lilly wouldn't have minded," I said.

She chuckled, but it wasn't a happy sound. "I doubt that," she said.

I loved Lilly after only the few hours spent in her company, so I was immediately defensive in her behalf. "Why would you say that? She's wonderful."

"Because she doesn't think all that highly of humans, especially human girls," she said as we started on the way home.

She hadn't seemed that way to me. "How do you know?" I asked.

She shrugged and said, "Rumors mostly. We lowly humans may be allowed into the community, but we aren't really in it. We stick together and share our woes and frustrations. Lady Lilly's name used to come up quite a bit. Not as much anymore, though. Not since her boys grew up and settled."

"Settled how?"

"Settled into marriages with humans. It's hard to condemn the intermingling of bloods when your children marry humans. Especially not if you want grandchildren and expect to have any type of relationship with them," she said.

She sounded bitter. "Peggy? Can I ask you something?"

"Sure, go ahead. What is there to really hide?" she asked.

"How do you fit into the community? It seems rude to ask, but since you aren't a shifter, you had to have been married in, right?" I asked.

"Yeah, I married a Staton. We have two boys, just like everyone else in the clan," she said.

"Are you happy?" I asked. I wanted to know if what Lilly had told me about the human women becoming infatuated with the men of their pairing was true.

"Yes, I love my husband very much," she said, her face softening.

"He's okay with you working outside the home?" I asked. Since my father had pretty much insisted my mother quit working once he came home, I wanted to know if that was also standard operating procedure for the wolves.

"Not really. We had a bit of a fight about it at first, but our children are grown and away at college. He is gone at work all day. I was lonely. It seemed like a good idea to get out and do something with all my time. It took a bit of convincing, but I finally got my way. It helped that your grandfather filled the job. I think that is the only reason I was allowed."

Allowed. That word stuck in my gut and made me mad. She was an adult – she shouldn't have to ask permission from anyone to do anything, and yet, there she was, *allowed* to get a job and make her own money. The world of the wolves continued to tick me off at every turn.

I was annoyed and didn't want to talk anymore. I wasn't really mad at her but at the injustice of the lives of females in our world, whether human or not. I hated it.

By the time we arrived home, I was exhausted. I went inside and although I wasn't really sneaking about, I tried to be quiet. I didn't want to run into anyone, especially any males that I was going to have to contend with. I grabbed a quick snack in the kitchen and then headed to my room, where I intended to stay until the dreaded harsh effects of my first heat wore down enough to be around people without consequences.

Chapter Nine

My plan to stay in my room lasted a whole night. I slept in the next day and woke up around noon, but I didn't want to waste my day holed up in my room. Alone. "Screw them," I said to myself and decided I was going outside whether they liked it or not.

I showered and dressed and walked proudly down the stairs to…an empty kitchen. "Figures," I said. I toasted a bagel, smothered it with cream cheese, and took it with me outside. I was a few miles from town, but I didn't mind the idea of walking it, or if I took the forest, I could get there quicker by running.

I left through the back door and headed straight into the forest. No one called after me, so I assumed no one knew where I was. Maybe they just didn't care, which wouldn't have surprised me one bit. I entered the forest and, as always, immediately felt calmer. The animal in me settled and my brain quieted.

That was where I belonged, just as much as I did with humans. I needed to spend more time doing things my wolf enjoyed as much as I did the human things of life, like school and shopping. Not that I had done much shopping lately, but still. The forest was part of me. I needed to remember that.

I finished off my bagel then began to jog my way through the forest. I didn't need trails to find my way. I wasn't worried about falling over tree roots or tripping on uneven ground. Even in my human form, I had the grace of the wolf. I picked up speed easily and made my way to my old home.

I hadn't consciously decided to go there, but that was where I ended up. I stepped out of the forest and looked at the place I had once called home. I saw it through new eyes. Not the eyes of a child happy to be home. Not the eyes of a teen enjoying the freedom of the world. No. I saw it through the eyes of an outcast. Through the eyes of an unwanted person, afraid to step through the creaky old gate for fear of being rebuked. I stared at my home and felt such oppressive sadness that I closed my eyes and had to turn away without going in.

"What are you doing?"

I opened my eyes. Brian stood in the shade of the forest just out of reach of the sunshine that still heated the day. "Nothing. Just thinking. What are you doing here? Why aren't you in school?"

"School's over today, Abby. It's like three o'clock," he said.

"Oh," I said in genuine surprise. I hadn't realized how late in the day it was. I guess that is what happens when you sleep half the day away.

"Did you go to school today?" he asked.

"No. I took a personal day," I said.

"You sick?"

I shook my head. "Just needed a day to myself." Yeah, more like a few weeks, apparently. How did girls get an education in this world of heats and hormones and smells and wolves? But on the bright side, at least I only had to deal with it twice a year, so it could be worse.

"I can understand that," he said. "So, do you want to go for a walk? With me?"

Did I? I looked back at my mother's house and realized I could use a bit of normal, and since Brian was as normal as they came, I took him up on his offer. "Sure. Why not?" I admit that I was feeling a little bit worried about it, only because we hadn't been on the best of terms the last few months, and he was getting weird when it came to all the so-called dogs, aka wolves, running around the place, but he was Brian. We'd been friends since birth. We grew up together and were best friends our whole lives. He wouldn't hurt me. Although I couldn't trust him with any of the wolf stuff, I could trust him with anything else. Right? Couldn't I?

We entered the quiet of the woods together. We were both silent for a while, but it was not an uncomfortable silence. After we had walked a ways, I asked, "How is school this year? You taking anything fun?"

"Same old stuff, just a new year. I did get Mrs. Green for lit class," he said.

"That's great," I replied. He'd wanted that teacher since freshman year. I was glad he finally got her.

"What about you? Anything exciting in the world of the privileged?" he said, his tone dripping with sarcasm.

"Brian," I said, "don't ruin it."

"You're right. I'm sorry," he said back in a normal tone.

"There isn't anything new or different at my school this year. It really is all the same stuff, just a different school. They don't have any clubs that I know of. Did you join art club this year or anything? I know you were thinking about it last year."

"Sort of," he said. "Look, that's what I wanted to talk to you about, why I asked you out here."

Just like that, with those few words, dread settled in the pit of my stomach. "Okay," I said evenly.

"Well, you see I did join a club of sorts," he said. "It's not through the school, though. It's an outside group that invited me in. I mentioned it to you before. Remember?"

"What kind of outside group invites strangers in?" I asked.

"It's a group called the Hunterz," he said.

The dread was turning into a full-on panic. I could feel my heart begin to pick up speed and race in my chest. "What exactly do they hunt? Like big game? Elephants and lions?" Please God, let them be something like that.

"No," he said and hesitated. "They hunt wolves."

I halted and turned to him. "Wolves? Do we have a wolf problem that I need to know about?"

He wrapped his hand around my elbow as if to hold me there in place. That immediately set me off, and I started to get mad.

"I think you already know of the wolf problem in our area," he said.

I twisted my arm and tried to give him the hint to let go, but he didn't take it. Instead, his grip tightened and he leaned in close to my face. "Let go. You're hurting me," I said.

"I need you to listen to me," he said. "I think you are in danger. Do you know what your father is? Do you know what most of the people going in and out of your house are? Tell me the truth this time, Abby."

I was thinking as fast as I could, trying to find a way to respond that would calm down the situation – it was getting out of control fast. "Umm, people," I said. Then I tried again, "Stop it, Brian, let go."

"No, Abby. They aren't just people. They're wolves," he said. His face was so sincere, so earnest, so worried and afraid.

I didn't know what to say to him. So I tried to go the calming route. "What are you talking about? You sound crazy."

"I mean it!" he yelled in my face. "I don't know how they do it, but they change or morph or whatever into animals."

I lowered my voice and whispered conspiratorially, "Did you see them do this? I mean really see it?"

"No. But the Hunterz, they told me all about it."

I laughed. Oh, it was forced on my part, but I played it up as well and as dramatic as I could. I held my belly with my one arm and said, "Oh, Brian. Geez, really? You know my mom and me. You have known us for years. We're just normal people. Why would you believe something so silly? Especially without any real proof. You can't go around accusing people of stuff like that. They must be playing with you, or making you into some kind of joke. You are smarter than that. Did they ask you for money?"

"It's not a joke," he said and shook my arm in anger, as if that would change my mind. "I think you're in danger."

"Why would I be in danger, and from who? My mother? What's she going to do to me?" I said, yanking my arm as hard as I could and finally freeing myself of his clamp-like hold. I thought about running, but that would only fuel his belief that he was correct in what he thought he knew about the wolves. I had to find a way to make him see reason, make him believe me instead of the Hunterz.

"I don't know, Abby, but they have documentation from like a hundred years back on this family of wolves. They are all over our area and have been for years. It's why they want you to go to their school, live in the big house with your so-called grandfather. They want to sacrifice you or something."

"Brian, stop it. You're acting crazy. No one is out to hurt me or sacrifice me. For God's sake, do you hear yourself? I live with my grandfather because I chose too. My father wanted me to stay there with him and my mother, but I don't want to. I left. I didn't ask anyone or get permission. I just left and moved. They would have me back in a second if I wanted to. Here's the thing – I don't want to."

"Maybe it's because you're just a girl," he said suddenly excited.

"Excuse me?" I said and eyeballed him with such disdain he could not have missed it. Apparently, he still did, though.

"I think they only have boy children, so only boys are the changer ones. Girls aren't important," he said as he paced before me.

I tried to stay calm by counting his steps. One, two, three steps in one direction. Then one, two, three, four in the other direction. Back and forth, the same steps. "Brian," I said, trying to get his attention, but he was too far gone within his own thoughts.

"So that would mean you and your mother are fine. You can't be the changers. And that means you aren't your father's real child. That's why he wanted you out of the house. That's why he never came around, and that is why you are going to be scarified. Oh, my God! Abby! That is it!" He took hold of my arm again and tried to drag me with him. "You have to come with me to the Hunterz. They will protect you."

I dug my feet into the ground and halted him, barely. "Brian, I am not going anywhere with you right now, especially not to some fanatical club place."

"Abby, you don't understand. I'm trying to protect you."

"From what? Some convoluted idea you have? You can't go around talking like this to people. They are going to think you have headed off into crazy town. Do you even hear yourself anymore?" I tried to get through to him.

"You have to listen," he said and jerked me forward again. I again pulled back to halt our progress.

"No, Brian. You have to listen to me. No one is out to sacrifice me. I promise."

"You just don't realize it yet," he said.

"My mother and father are not going to hurt me, and yes, he is my real father. Brian, stop," I said when he turned away and began to physically drag me in the direction he wanted to go. I was getting ticked off and trying to stay calm so that I could get through to him.

"Then tell me this?" he said. "Why haven't I seen your mother around lately? What happened to her?"

"You do realize my mother is pregnant, right?" I said thinking that would get through to him. Make him see that she was just a woman.

"Pregnant?" he said quietly.

"She's really sick with this baby. They told me she was the same way with me in the beginning. She is spending a lot of time in bed. They are trying to just get through this period with her. She's not gone, Brian. I can show you if you need to see her." I hoped I was correct in thinking I would be allowed to let him see her. Who knew what the wolves would do if I tried to bring a human, a male human, into the house at this point.

"She's having one of them! That's why she is so sick," he said.

"No. No, Brian, she was sick like that with me too," I implored him to hear me.

"We have to kill it," he said.

That was it. I snapped. I grabbed him by his collar, and using my wolf strength I yanked him to within a millimeter of my face and said through clenched teeth, "What did you just say? You did not just threaten to kill a baby did you? My own brother or sister? I did not just hear that, right?"

I don't know if I was all that scary to Brian. I was just a girl, after all. But if he only knew how close to violence I was at that moment, he would have been.

He pulled free easily enough, only because I let him, but then he surprised me by taking both my upper arms into his hands and shaking me back and forth like a bowl of Jello. "It will be one of them! We have to!" he shouted at me all the while.

I went from mad to scared when I saw the blurred crazy swirling in his eyes. I started to sweat in the fear that he really would set out to hurt my mother or the baby. I wasn't happy about the baby, for my own reasons, but I wasn't mad at the baby itself and I would never let

99

anyone or anything hurt it. Brian was about to find out how serious I was. When he yanked me forward, I grabbed hold of his arms and held myself in place. Then I jerked my knee up into his crotch. It took all of two seconds to see his angry face turn to one of shock and then pain. He let go of me immediately and held onto himself instead as he bowed over his knees and moaned as if he were dying.

I grabbed a handful of the hair at the back of his head and jerked it back so that he could see my face. "Don't you ever threaten my family again. Do you hear me?"

He was seething with rage behind the pain, but I refused to be a coward in the face of it. I held onto my own fear and waited for his response. It came through teeth clenched so tight I was surprised I could even hear him. "Yes, I hear you."

"Good. Go home, Brian," I said and turned away from him.

"Abby," he said. I halted and looked over my shoulder at him. "If you could only come and talk to them, I think you would understand why I'm scared."

I wasn't going to go anywhere with him. However, I wanted him to have time to calm down. "I'll think about it if…"

"If, what?" he said.

"If you think about what I am saying. You can't be taken in by these people, Brian. You have to realize they sound crazy and so do you. Don't go back to them. I'm afraid for you."

He was standing upright again. Some of the rage was gone from his face, but there was definitely something wild still there. "And I'm afraid for you," he said. "Can't you see that?"

"I need to get home," I said. "I will think about what you said. You do the same."

I walked away from him. I was afraid that if I said anything else, he would go off the deep end again and I didn't think I could control myself anymore around him if he did. I used my wolf senses to smell the air and see around me and hear all that was going on in the woods. When I was certain I was alone, I shifted to my wolf, without care for my clothes or anything. I needed to get home. I needed to talk to my grandfather.

I ran hard and fast, but it was still dark by the time I arrived home. I walked right in, thanks to a held open door, and padded my way through the kitchen. Before I could get to my room to change and get dressed, I was halted by the angry voice and words of my grandfather.

"Where have you been?" he demanded, but before I could have tried to respond, he continued with, "Just because I am not your parent doesn't mean you can run off all day and not check in. I won't have your disrespect young lady! Now go to your room!"

Fine! That was where I wanted to be anyway! I would talk to him tomorrow. It would keep for the night. Maybe he would be in a better mood. Then, just to make sure he understood that I heard him but was not all that thrilled with his tone and anger with me, as I walked past him I turned my head and snarled an ugly sound of hate. I tried to remember that part of his problem was due to my hormones going nuts inside of me, but it was hard. It wasn't my fault after all. Maybe if he had balanced with his wolf he wouldn't be having such a problem in my presence.

That thought stayed on my mind as I headed upstairs for the night. I should be hungry, but worry ate away inside me and took away my appetite.

Chapter Ten

The next day began as the one before it had. I woke up and went downstairs to find myself alone. I was getting pretty sick and tired of always being alone. I headed outside and found Alex. The moment the fall breeze picked up, he stiffened and turned to where I stood behind him. His expression was partly fear and partly shame. I didn't have time for either one. "I need you to take me to see my grandfather." When he didn't immediately respond, I said, "Now."

"Miss, he is at work and not to be disturbed. I am not able to take you," he said.

"Fine. Then take me to my father," I said not giving an inch. "Look, it's kind of important, so let's get a move on." I turned on my heel and stomped to the car, where I ended up having to wait for him to come to terms with my demand. Finally, I saw his shoulders visibly sag, but he did as instructed. He rolled down the windows, all of them in the car. It would have been funny had it been someone else, but the fact that I smelled so bad, or in this case, so good, that he had to get fresh air, made me a bit uncomfortable. I dreaded the reception I would get from my father.

We left the small town and made it into the city, where we pulled up to a tall building that said Staton Financial in big blue letters across the front. What exactly did the family do? "I thought my father was in construction or something," I said.

"No," Alex said, but that was all.

I exited the car on my own and stood in front of the big building. Now that I was there, I wasn't sure what to do or where to go. I turned back to the car and leaned down to speak through the window, "You'll wait for me, right?"

"Yes," he said. "I'll watch for you to come out. I'll have to find a place to park, but I won't leave." His tone was clipped and short, but it wasn't mean. He was trying to do his job all the while fighting his wolf because of me. This heat thing was complicated. How did the girls handle it in the past?

"Okay," I said. I gathered some courage and entered the building. There was a young woman sitting at a desk about ten feet inside the doors. I walked directly over to her and said, "I'd like to see Adam Staton."

She looked me up and down, with her steely blue eyes and high-unimpressed eyebrows, and said, "And you are?"

I was nobody, but I still needed to see him. "Abigail Staton, his daughter," I said with smug sarcasm.

Her fake smile stayed in place but became stiff and unsure. Good, maybe she wouldn't judge people on their first impression next time. "Just one moment. I will announce you."

I set my arms on the little counter and leaned against it. Obviously waiting and listening to her stilted discussion on the phone with who, I assumed, was a secretary or assistant of some kind. I watched her all the while and thought meanly that maybe if her dark brown, almost black, hair wasn't so tightly pulled back in such a neat and tidy bun that maybe she would be in a better mood. That must be giving her a headache.

She set down the phone and said, "They will be waiting for you. You can go up to the seventh floor. Amanda will greet you."

"Great," I said and turned toward the elevators just to the left of her. "Thanks."

I rode up the elevator in silence. There was no cheeky music playing, nothing but the whirling and grinding of the motor and cables to break up the emptiness. The interior was all mirrors. I glanced at myself and thought that maybe I should have taken a bit more care in my appearance that morning. I hadn't realized I would be going into such a swanky business. There were too many secrets in the family. This office was one of them. So instead, I arrived at the office in a stressed pair of jeans and a simple tank top. I hadn't even layered it with anything. My hair was, yeah, it was the usual unruly mess. I tried to quickly pat it down, but that didn't do any good.

The elevator stopped and the doors opened up into a grand waiting room. Waiting just outside the doors was a tidy woman with a big toothy smile on her face. She reached out her hand to me as she said, "You must be Abigail." She didn't give me a moment to agree or disagree. She instead continued to talk as I shook her hand out of expectation rather than desire. "I'm Amanda, your father's assistant. Come with me. I have the conference room set up for you. Your father will meet you there directly." She turned and walked briskly down a long, very bright hallway. She stopped and showed me into a room to the left.

"Can I get you anything? Coffee?" she asked. Her eyebrows were huge. I noticed as one was raised up expectantly. She was in a stern gray suit and wore little matching gray pumps. Her brown hair was short, way short, but it didn't look horrible thanks to her tiny little face. Efficient. That was the word that came to mind when you looked at her.

"No," I said. "I'm good."

"I'll just get your father then," she said and was gone.

I was uncomfortable in the large room. Maybe it was the huge multi-chaired table that took up the bulk of the space that made me feel that way. Why had she brought me there to this room? I walked to the large picture window and stared out over the city. Fog hung low and blurred some of the view, but otherwise, it was nice.

My father strode into the room, without so much as a hello. Instead he got right to the point, "What are you doing here?"

"Well, hello to you too. It's nice to see you," I said as I crossed my arms over my chest while I stared at him.

Adam Staton was a good-looking man, especially all decked out in his black suit and green tie. Yes, very handsome. I could see why my mother was attracted to him at first sight. "Fine. Hello. Now, what do you want?"

I had so much to talk to him about that was very important, or at least I thought it might be, but I had to ask something first before I started into the Hunterz and Brian problem. "Why do you hate me?"

He seemed surprised by my question. Maybe it had been the tone of abject sorrow, which I had not planned for but came through anyway, that had gotten his attention. "I don't hate you," he said. Then he turned and quietly shut the door.

"You act like you do," I said. "Can't you ever say anything nice or just try to be nice? Do you only save the good parts of yourself for my mother? Because I sure as heck have never seen it for myself."

"You mother is easy to love," he said. "She is giving and wants to receive. You aren't. You look for deception in every movement, in every said word. You want to hate. It makes you feel better. I understand that, but then you can't be upset when I return your disdain with the same. I don't want to fight you."

My mother was easy to love. He was right about that. The rest, I didn't know what to think. Was I the one keeping the animosity going between us? I didn't want to be thrown away by him. So maybe I kept my distance and the awkwardness going in order to make sure that didn't happen, or if and when it did, I would expect it so it wouldn't hurt so badly. Maybe this really was my fault. I wasn't about to admit that to him, though. Not yet. I needed to think about it some more, when I didn't have other more pressing matters to deal with.

So, I changed the subject without notice and asked, "What are the Hunterz?"

I saw the wolf in him come to attention. It was in the perk of his ears. It was the direct stare in his eyes. It was the flare of his nostrils. It was in the dark tone of his voice when he asked with deadly calm, "Where did you hear that name?"

"Who are they? What do they want?" I asked instead of answering him.

"They are a group that I thought had finally been disbanded. I haven't heard of them since I was…since I was about your age. That was the last time they reared their ugly, perverted head."

I pulled out a chair and sat down. "I think they have recruited, Brian." When he didn't seem to know who that was, I said, "The boy next door?"

"How do you know?" he asked.

"We had a…discussion last night. He wanted me to go with him to meet them. He has it in his head that you and the rest of the evil wolves are going to sacrifice me." I didn't want to tell him the part about mom and the baby, but I felt I had to. What if Brian and his Hunterz did something to hurt her or the baby? I would never forgive myself. "There is something else, but you can't freak out, okay?"

He sat down across from me and said, "I can't promise you that. I'm having a hard enough time being shut up in this room with you right now. My wolf is clamoring inside me. I'm already a bit hyped up."

He said it so nonchalantly that for a moment I was confused. He didn't appear to be struggling with the animal inside. In fact, he appeared calm and serene as he sat there in front of me with his hands clasped on the table. Then again, his hands were clenched rather tightly, and since I was looking for signs, his eyes were squinty. Then there was the tiniest almost unnoticeable hunch of his shoulders. Okay, maybe he was struggling a bit, but seriously, had he not mentioned it, I would not have known it.

"I can't change my bodily functions right now. You are just going to have to deal with it as this is important," I said.

He nodded his head at me in agreement and said, "I will try not to…freak out, as you put it."

I was afraid to say it out loud. Saying it out loud made it real. Made it possible. I took a deep breath and tried to stay calm like he appeared to be, and said, "I think mom and the baby may be in danger."

I watched my father closely for signs of added emotion. I wasn't disappointed. He hands turned white at the knuckles from where his grip tightened enormously. His breathing increased and became labored, as if he was having trouble pulling air into his lungs. Then, as if he gave up the fight, he jerked to his feet. The chair he had been sitting in was flung backward and slammed into the wall behind him. He slammed the palms of his hands down on the table with such force that the sound of the smack echoed around me in the empty room. "What do you mean she may be in danger?"

He didn't mention the baby part, which made me even surer that he did in fact love my mother, very much. It was apparently just the children he had a bit of trouble connecting with.

I stood up and leaned toward him over the big table and tried to shush him. "Calm down. You said you wouldn't freak out."

"This is your mother we are talking about. She will not be hurt," he said as if he could simply decree it and it would be done.

"Sit down and let me tell you what I know," I said. I could tell he wanted to throw things or shake me or just maybe punch the wall, but instead, he turned rather stiffly, pulled the chair back toward the table and sat down. He stared at me and waited for me to continue.

"Brian believes that only the boys can be shifters, and that only boys can be born to shifters. So, that means I am safe. He thinks I am not your biological daughter. Not that you were worried about me or anything," I said just a tiny bit sarcastically, "but I think I'm safe in the scheme of things. But mom, he first thought you had done something to her and that she was either chained up somewhere or dead. I told him no, that she was pregnant and sick, which caused him to have a mini-coronary."

"Why would you tell him she was with child?" he said. His face was red and he was back to clenching his hands together.

"I didn't know he would flip out. I was trying to show him how normal we are, that we couldn't be these creatures. We were just a normal family making babies and all that good stuff. How was I to know he was going to believe mom is possessed and is the incubus to your evil prodigy and either she must be killed to save her, or the baby needs to be?"

"This is bad," he said, not really to me but more in general to himself.

"Well, if someone had warned me or thought to simply tell me this was a problem, I could have been prepared. But no, just like every other major event lately, it's all some big gigantic secret that I have to find out after the fact."

"I think I need some air," he said.

It was my turn to get mad. I got his attention by slamming my own palm down on the table just as he had. When he swung around to look at me, I said, "Get your wolf under control! I don't have time for this smelling heat thing to be in the way. I can't help it. Suck it up, pull it together, and tell me what we need to do!"

The expression on his face was one of shock and surprise and there around the edges was a bit of pride. Where did that come from and what did it mean? He liked me being a raving wench? Wolves are so…confusing. I mean seriously confusing.

"That wasn't quite what I meant. Yes, your...scent is a bit overpowering in here and it is upsetting my wolf. I needed air because I need to think what to do. We have to protect your mother."

He said 'we.' He was including me. He was even listening to me. Even with all that was going on, even with all my worry, my heart did a little dance inside my chest with that one little expression of togetherness. "I am so messed up," I said to myself.

"What?" he said.

"Nothing," I replied. "So what do we do?"

He stood up and went to stand by the window, as I had done earlier. "I think maybe since your mother is sick with the baby we shouldn't tell her what is going on. I also think that will be the perfect excuse to move her into the safety of my father's home. They can't get in there. Not without some serious power."

"Move her into grandfather's...with me?" Why that suddenly brought absolute fear and dread into my heart, I had no idea. It just did.

"Yes, temporarily," he said decidedly and firmly. "We will do so this evening. Immediately."

"Don't you think you should talk to grandfather first?" I said, hedging for time.

"He will agree. I will confirm after we are finished up here," he said. He stood up, pushed in his chair and said, "We are done here, right? You didn't have any other bombs to drop on me today did you?"

He sounded almost like he was trying to tease me, but it didn't quite make it to that level, so I was unsure how to respond. "No. That was all," I said.

"Good. I'll have Amanda show you down," he said.

"I'm sure I can figure it out myself. It's just down that hallway."

He actually smiled. Not big and joyous, but it was still a smile. Maybe things weren't as bad between us as I thought.

109

"I'm sure you can," he said. He hesitated at the door then blurted out, "Thank you for coming in today and telling me what was on your mind."

I'd gotten a smile and a thank you from him all in the span of sixty seconds. The day just got weird. "You are welcome?" I said, but it came out a question as if I wasn't entirely sure myself.

At the door, he turned one way and I turned the other. "Have a good rest of your day," he said over his shoulder.

"You too," I said. Did he even hear me? I had been dismissed as quickly as I had appeared. I wasn't as upset about it as I would have been, though. I followed his back as he turned out of sight at the end of the hallway. Maybe he wasn't as bad as I made him out to be. Maybe. I wasn't sold on the idea yet, but maybe there was hope. What always threw me off with him was that he was good to my mother. I could see the affection between them, and it seemed real. I knew he had some good inside him. It simply hadn't been shown in my direction much.

I pushed the button for the elevator and thought about my father. He had once sent me those beautiful music globe boxes. I always wondered if they were for me or really for my mother. He still sent them. They were hand crafted. They were expensive. Maybe…

I left the building and looked around for the car with Alex. It was halfway down the block waiting. There was nothing all that unusual about that. What took me by surprise was that Derek was there, leaning against the door, his arms crossed over his chest.

I headed in that direction. He was definitely a good-looking guy. Too bad he had a bad case of male chauvinism in him.

He wore a short-sleeved, black t-shirt that showed his biceps in a grand display. As I got closer, I saw that the t-shirt was maybe a size too small, as it stretched its way across his heavily muscled chest. Had he gotten bigger in the last few months? Because wow.

I cleared my suddenly tight throat before I asked, "What are you doing here?" It sounded rude even before all the words left my lips.

Thankfully he didn't take it the way it sounded, or he didn't appear to. He did, however, raise an eyebrow at me when he said, "Your father called me. Asked me to ride with you to the house and make sure you made it there safe."

"When did he do that? I just left his office," I asked.

He shrugged and then said, "Come on. Let's get out of here." He opened the door and waved me in, and then we were off and headed home.

I looked at him from the side of my eye. He seemed to be in a pretty decent mood. He was leaning a little bit into the air coming in from all the windows still being down, but otherwise, he seemed pretty relaxed.

"Can I ask you something?" I asked

"Sure," he said, but I didn't really have his attention. He didn't look at me, but out the window as the scenery passed.

I asked anyway, "What do you know about the Hunterz?"

That got his attention. He swung his head around. "Why?"

I heaved a great and pained sigh. "Doesn't anyone just answer questions around here? God! They are around, and I need to know who they are and what they want. So just freaking tell me, or if you don't know, then tell me who I need to talk to."

He sat back and again turned to watch out the window. I had begun to get mad that he was going to ignore my question when he finally said, "I don't know all that much about them, just what you hear in rumors or whispered conversations. The older generation doesn't talk about it."

"Surprise," I said.

He put his hand on my leg to shush me, but he didn't remove it when I fell still and silent. He kept it there. I lost my train of thought for a moment as I focused on the heat coming off his huge paw of a hand. Why was it so warm?

He drew my attention back to the conversation though when he said, "They are murderers. Or so everyone says. I guess they started out as a trusted group of men that were hired to get the wolves through those first few years of torment. Keep the wolves safe while they learned to control themselves and the curse."

"Gift," I said interrupting him. It wasn't a curse, and until they saw that, they would never find balance.

"Do you want to hear this or not?" he said.

"Yes, sorry. Go on," I said, chastised.

"This is all just information I have picked up over the years. I believe the first Hunterz was the best friend of Sirus, the first of the wolves. He was your great, great, great, grandfather."

"I know who he is," I said.

"Well, from what I can tell, he confided in his friend. His friend then stood by his side and helped him through the rough years. Especially the full moon times when Sirus was forced to shift."

"So what happened? Why did they turn against us?"

"Sirus had children who in turn became wolves at puberty who had children and so on and so on. The friend of Sirus then brought in his children to help and their children to help. The clan and the Hunterz grew in number over the years until there were many of each."

"What happened?" I asked again.

"It is believed that they became jealous of the wolves. We don't age the same as humans. We are stronger, more powerful. We are also mentally superior. I'm not saying that humans are stupid. I'm just stating a fact that we are smarter."

"Anyway," I said to move him along. I wasn't going to get into an intelligence argument with him right then.

"They demanded we change them into what we were in exchange for their silence. It was all coming to a head when one of the wolves fell in love with one of the Hunterz and the union was forbidden. The two were separated. The girl was heartbroken and her family angry. Tensions between the families grew. The tension turned to anger, and that anger soon turned to rage. They began to hunt us. They deemed us evil, one of Satan's creatures that needed to be destroyed. There was never a big battle to speak of. They would just hunt for us. If they found one alone or sick, they would kill us."

"Did we kill any of them?" I asked.

"I'm sure we did. It's been how many years? A hundred? Two? It's a war that was created by jealousy. You can't stem the flow of jealousy. We beat it back now and then, and think we have them beaten, but they continue to rear their head when we least expect it."

"Why now?" I asked, not really expecting an answer, but I got one anyway.

"Why not? We thought their sick little group had fizzled out. There has been no contact with them for years and years. So no one is expecting them to show up. This is the time to attack us, when we are least prepared."

"We should warn the Grey clan. They need to know we're all in danger," I said.

He made a growling sound. I took it to mean he was not really in agreement with me, but he wasn't going to fight me on it either. It didn't matter in the end because when we pulled up to the house, there in the front yard was my group of boys from the Grey side. They were sitting on the front walkway and lounging in the yard. Apparently they had not been allowed inside. Not that I was surprised.

I jumped out of the car and ran over to them, happy to see their faces, until I remembered what the last meeting had been like. I halted several feet back from them, suddenly wary of the reception. "Hey

113

guys," I said. It was more a way to break the quiet than anything else. Besides, I was suddenly shy and not sure what else to say, along with embarrassed.

"Hey, Abby," Max said.

I glanced over the small group of boys. All of them looked well, except for Oscar. His hand was bandaged thick with white gauze. "Did I do that?" I asked. Everyone knew what I was talking about. I didn't need to point and explain.

Oscar shrugged. "I think I deserved it."

Dillon stepped forward and said, "Look, Abby. We wanted to come and see how you were and tell you how sorry we are about what happened. We didn't know that would happen. I could tell you that it wasn't really our fault because no one warned us about a female's…"

I cringed at what I knew was coming. It was embarrassing to me. Every single guy in both clans would always know when I was about to be on my period. What was worse, they all knew when I was fertile, and that was no one's business, and yet, apparently it was in the air for all to know.

"…heat. We didn't know anything about it."

"Yeah, join the crowd," I said. "Look, guys, we were all taken a bit off guard. Why don't we just forget it? I won't mention the incident as long as you all forget that I went a little blood wild there on Oscar."

"I'm not mad," Oscar said. He came forward and opened his arms to give me a hug. I stepped forward to return the embrace, but was halted in my steps by a firmly clamped hand on my elbow. I turned annoyed eyes to Derek and said, "Hey."

He didn't look at me though. His eyes were like ice on the little pack of Grey boys. A low rumbling in his chest warned of his agitation.

"Derek." I physically pulled his face down so he would look at me.

"This is not a good time to get in close personal space of other males," he said.

"I'm in close personal space with you," I said. "You seem to do all right."

"They didn't before. Why would they now?" he said.

That was a very good question. I turned back to the others and said, "He has a point."

Max stepped forward and said, "We were taken by surprise. We didn't know. We're now aware of the problem and have taken steps to not have it happen again. You can come back to school. We will keep you safe."

Derek again growled and bared his teeth. "She will return to school when it is deemed she is safe. Not when you tell us she is."

I sighed. It was always the same with the Staton men. They would get all controlling and jerky. I looked from the little group of guys to Derek and said firmly and loudly, "I will return to school when I deem it is safe. When I feel like it. Not when anyone else says I can or tells me too. You all got that?"

I bore my stare into each individual guy to be sure they could understand that I was serious. I wasn't putting up with the whole 'girls are weak and must be protected' crap.

"Abby, they're not safe," Derek said. He wasn't quiet about it either. He wanted them to hear him accuse them. "They proved it to you already once this week."

He got the reaction he wanted. The small group puffed up and was angry just like that. The male testosterone flying around me was almost overwhelming. Then I realized that I might have been the reason tempers were set to go off. My own hormones were all around us. I quickly stepped further back from the males and said, "Everyone take a step back. We're all antsy and I think it's maybe my fault."

Derek jerked his eyes to me. I could see the dawning realization of what was going on. Oh, my God, for once Derek believed me. Hell must have frozen over. The Grey boys took a bit longer to settle down and accept the idea, though. I realized that maybe there was something to be said for the control of the Statons. The Greys did lack in it. It was most evident for the first time right there.

"Guys, look. I'm not really good company for anyone right now. None of you really have control of the animals within you. None." I looked directly at Derek. He had more control, but I could still see him struggling inside. His anger showed it the most. "Until I get through the first phase of this…thing, I think I'm better left on my own."

"But," Max said.

I was shaking my head at them, stopping any of their responses. "I can't be the one that causes fighting among you all. I think until you guys balance with your wolves, it's dangerous. I think that's what you should be worrying about. The wolves are fighting to get out and you are fighting to keep them in. Both parts need to stop."

"What is that going to change, Abby?" Max asked. "Even if we find this balance you keep talking about, we are still going to be out of whack when you're like this."

"I think that is the point. I'm beginning to think that once you do come together with your wolves, any issues you have with me in this stage won't matter. I wish you guys could understand how it is with me now. I'm whole. I am human and I am wolf, together as one. You guys are broken in half on the inside. Neither part of you is in control. You are always fighting within yourselves. All your energy is spent fighting. Once you come together, there is nothing left to fight. You will be in control of all things, whether in this form or in wolf."

They were looking at me with such confusion that I knew they couldn't understand right then. I got mad and frustrated. "Look. I smell great and both you as a human want me and you as a wolf want me.

116

You are both fighting each other for who wants me more. Look at Dillon. He won't admit it, but he is more focused within trying to keep full control of staying human than he is on anything else. If I were to entice him in the slightest…"

"Abby," Derek growled. I thought he might have an idea of what I was about to do. He wouldn't like it, but I was going to make my point, one way…or another.

I used my hips and my shoulders to appear sexy. I softened my face and my eyes, to appear fragile. Then I took a slow step in Dillon's direction. I lowered my voice into a seductive tone and said, "I don't think it will take much." I slowly licked my lips, all the while staring and giving my full attention to him.

I was still several feet back when his wolf burst forward and he shifted. Bits and pieces of his clothing flew out in a burst of confetti. He crouched low on the ground and prepared to pounce as the pieces drifted down around him like snow. It was that fast. It had taken him less than a full minute to lose it.

The others tackled him quickly before he could try to seize me. I wasn't certain what he would do if he did get a hold of me like that, but I didn't want to find out. Apparently neither did anyone else, as Dillon was quickly subdued and held down by the weight of the others, all but Derek, who'd stayed almost directly behind me the entire time.

"See?" I said dropping all pretense of seduction. "He was so busy fighting to contain his wolf and his wolf was so busy fighting to get out, that he couldn't stop himself. You guys have to balance."

"That was stupid," Derek said in my ear.

I wasn't about to let him bully me right then. "You guys have to figure this out. Get mad at me all you like, but that just proves that all your control is nothing but an illusion. All of you need to figure it out."

Chapter Eleven

I wasn't mad, but they may have thought I was. I turned on my heel, stomped my way inside, and slammed the door shut behind me. No, I wasn't angry. I didn't want to admit it out there, but I was a little unnerved at how quickly Dillon lost it. They had no control, no matter what they said. There was one question that still rattled around in my head, though: why did Derek seem to be maybe not great in my presence, but not chaotic either like the rest of the males.

For the next few days, I stayed in, hiding in my room for most of the day. My father, good to his word, moved my mother, and they were busy setting up a little suite-like section on the top floor for her and my father for the time being. I wanted to go up and see how they were doing and also what they were doing, but I stayed safe in my room away from all the chaos.

No one came to see me either. I could hear them through the ceiling. I was channeling my wolf hearing, but all the same, I could hear them. There was scraping along the floor and bumps and slams throughout the house. What were they doing up there? How much crap did they bring? It was only temporary, right?

When the noise finally went silent, my curiosity got the better of me. I stepped out of my room and tiptoed my way up to the third floor. I stepped carefully and quietly along the hallway as I tried to make my way up to mom's suite.

I could see light coming from one of the rooms and hear the murmur of voices. When I heard a very audible moan and the sound of running feet, I didn't know what to expect. My mother bolted out of the doorway with her hair streaming long out behind her and slammed her way into the bathroom across the hall. When the sound of retching reached my ears, I scrunched up my nose and figured I should come back another time. I turned and headed back to my solitary room.

"Alone again," I said to the empty room. I wanted to go out and run. I wanted to feel the crisp night air on my face. I didn't go, though. I was suddenly afraid to leave the house at night. There were all sorts of dangers out there that hadn't been there before. Not just the threat of Brian but any male wolf. I wished I would just start my period already and get this whole thing done. Plus since I hadn't even known what it was, I wasn't watching for it. Was this week one or week two? Was it almost over yet?

There were so many great and wonderful things about being a wolf. This was not one of them. I wished I had someone to talk too. I thought about calling Aunt Lilly. That sounded weird even in my head. She wasn't really the aunt type. She truly was Lady Lilly. I didn't think I could reconcile her to any other name. I glanced at my clock. Was ten too late to telephone? Maybe I could text? No, I highly doubted she knew how to text. I dug out my phone and saw that no one had tried to reach me either. I hadn't looked at my phone all day long and yet no one had texted me, and no one had called. Yes, alone again.

~ * ~

I growled in the darkness of my bedroom as I sat up. Why couldn't I sleep? It was…I squinted in the darkness to zero in on the clock across the room. It was not quite three in the morning, but it was close. I tossed off my blankets and stood to look out my window. The moon wasn't very big. In fact, there was hardly any moon at all.

119

I could see the wind blowing the leaves that circled and danced on the lawn below. I suddenly wanted to feel it. I was awake, so why not? What was there to be afraid of, really? I wasn't going to let some unknown threat take over my life. I wasn't!

Without turning on any lights, I found my flip-flops and slid them on. Then on silent feet I slipped out of my room and down the back stairs to the kitchen where I slipped out the back door.

Once outside, I ran just because it felt so good. It was partly the sneaking outside. It was partly the night and the darkness. Most of all, though, it was the freedom I felt running toward the forest.

I stopped just before entering the trees. I closed my eyes, tilted my head up, and breathed. The breeze lifted my hair off my neck and danced it around my head and face. I wanted to let out the wolf and run wild. I kicked off my shoes. I pulled off my t-shirt and flung it behind me. I reached for the hem of my tank top, but before I could whip it over my head to join my shirt, my eyes snapped open and my head jerked to the left.

I'd heard something, something big, maybe more than one something. I dropped down to a crouch and breathed in the air, trying to smell whatever it was. I didn't smell anything out of the ordinary. I tried again, but the results were the same. I began to think I just imagined the danger when I heard the snap of a twig in the other direction.

There was something out there. I quieted my mind, strained my ears and listened to the forest. There was something digging in the dirt. I could hear its feet as it scratched and pawed at the ground. I breathed in and realized it was a fox out hunting. That wasn't what I'd heard, though. It was too far to the center. I tried again and found squirrels high in the trees, one lumbering opossum, and several raccoons wandering the forest floor.

I knew there was danger out there in the woods, but I couldn't smell it and I couldn't see it. I pressed my ears and tried to push out all the normal wood sounds. I strained to hear the wrong sounds within the forest.

I was about to give up when I heard it. It was faint, and I almost didn't hear it at all. It was the sound of shiny leather, the sound it makes at the bend of an elbow or the rise of an arm. I used the directional sound and found there were other quiet noises, like the careful setting of feet on the ground. Not careful enough, though, as the leaves under their feet still crinkled enough for me to hear. There was the sound of breathing. It was slow and steady, but there it was. I smelled the air and still found nothing.

I couldn't smell them, but I could hear them. How were they masking their scent from me? How did they know they needed to? What were they doing in our forest?

I sensed the danger they posed and the hair on the back of my neck went stiff. Still in a crouch I frog-walked backward several steps, my eyes keen and focused on the forest. How many were there? I felt like I needed to know, but without being able to sense their individual smells, I couldn't tell.

My head whipped around to the other side when I realized there were more over on that side too. I'd heard the sound of brittle fall leaves as something or someone brushed against them. I backed up a few more steps. My heart was beating fast and hard in my chest. It was loud inside me and blocked out other noise and sounds that I may have heard. I tried to calm. I tried to slow it down. I wanted to shift to wolf. I would be stronger and faster in that form, but I didn't know how close the danger or if they could see me. There was enough danger of being found out without giving them something to film or see to prove they were right.

Fear trickled down my spine. How close were they? I needed to run. I needed to get inside. I turned my head to see how far to the house it really was. It was a long way. Could I run to it fast enough? Could I outpace the danger?

I decided to take the chance. I jumped to my feet and in the same breath, bolted for the house and the back door. I ran like I was being chased, and for all I knew, I was. I ran so hard my chest hurt. I pumped my arms as I ran. I ran so fast I hardly felt the cool grass on my bare feet. I hurled up the stairs and in the same motion threw open the door and fell inside. I slammed the big door closed and bolted it.

I dropped flat on my back on the floor and gasped for breath. My heart beat like it was trying to get out of my chest. I settled a hand on my chest and tried to slow my breathing and my heart.

I was almost back to normal when the overhead light winked on and blinded me.

"What the hell is going on? Abigail? What are you doing down here?"

My father, of course, towered over me. It had to be him, of all people. My eyes slowly adjusted to the light and I squinted up at him. I didn't get a chance to answer as his eyes were focused on my feet. My mud and grass covered feet. Oh crap, I was in trouble. My slowing heart picked up speed again.

"You were not just outside, were you?" he asked. It was not a question. It was a statement said with deadly calm. He already knew the answer. He just needed to say it out loud.

Since I was happy to have made it back inside alive, I wasn't all that afraid. Well, maybe I was a little because who wouldn't be? He was a big man with a bit of an animal temper. I answered him, "Yes."

He bent over me, grabbed my shoulders and hauled me up to my feet in a single motion. He didn't let go of me, though, oh, no. Instead, he pulled me up off the floor so my feet were no longer touching it and

I was level with his face. He asked with that same calm, which was completely contradictory to his actions at the time, "Why were you outside, Abigail?"

I swear I about peed myself. I half wanted to run back outside. At least the danger out there would have probably killed me quickly. "I...I wanted to run in the forest. I couldn't sleep. I thought the run would wear me out."

It was the truth, the whole truth, and yet, I doubted he believed me. There was something in his eyes that told me he didn't.

With extreme gentleness he set me back down on my feet. He turned away from me and said, "Go to bed. I don't want to look at you right now."

"I'm not lying to you," I said.

"We will discuss it in the morning," was his only reply.

"Fine, don't believe me," I said. I held my head up and proudly left the room. Yes, maybe going out in the middle of the night hadn't been all that smart, but it wasn't for any bad reason. I wasn't sneaking to meet anyone.

I snorted at that thought. Heck, if I wanted a guy right then, all I had to do was crook my little finger in his direction and he would come running to me. I didn't have to do any running, not with the way I smelled. The thought made me crinkle my nose. Smell, such a simple thing, but it grossed me out. I wanted to smell good in a conventional way, not a hormonal way.

I didn't really want a guy anyway. Did I? Derek's face flashed in my mind. No, no. I didn't want him. He was a controlling ass and, heck, he didn't even believe in love. I didn't want him. Even telling myself that, though, I knew I was lying. Maybe what I needed to remind myself was that I didn't want to want him.

I flopped back into my bed, dirty feet and all. I didn't care. I'd get the sheets changed in the morning. Part of the reason I didn't want

Derek was that my parents wanted me to. It was a stupid reason, but that was a big one. I was the keeper of my own destiny. No, he was not suitable. Just no.

Stupid Derek and his stupid gorgeous face were my last thoughts before I finally allowed sleep to claim me.

~ * ~

Morning came much too quickly to suit me. I guess that is what happens when you spend half the night tossing and turning and the other half running around outside. It was a good thing I wasn't going to school. Again. I was going to be so freaking far behind at this rate. Maybe I should see if I could get my work sent home to me. Maybe Derek wouldn't mind getting it. I growled at my traitorous thoughts and myself for even thinking them.

I rolled out of bed and began the day. I left my room after getting dressed and cleaned up. I dropped the dirty sheets from my bed in a pile in the hallway. I had no idea where to take them or if I was allowed to do anything with them. I went down to the kitchen to hunt down Peggy.

"Just leave them there. I'll get them when I clean up the second level," she said.

"I don't mind doing it. It's just laundry. I've done it before." Heck, I'd been helping with the laundry since I was big enough to reach the knobs. Besides, it felt funny to have my laundry being done by a virtual stranger.

"No, leave it. Really," she said and dismissed me by walking away.

"Okay then," I said as I headed off to find something to eat. Sadly, my father was in the kitchen when I got there.

"Why are you home?" I asked by way of greeting.

"It's Saturday," he said.

It was? Not going to school was throwing off my days. It was Saturday all ready? "Oh," I said.

"I want to speak to you about last night," he said.

"Yeah, I want to talk to you too," I said. "I think someone was in the forest last night."

"You don't say," he said. He picked up his cup of coffee and sipped it while his eye bore into me.

"Not me," I said. "Someone that didn't belong there. Someone sneaking around."

"There seems to be quite a bit of sneaking around going on around here," he said completely blowing me and my concerns off.

"I'm serious," I said trying to make him listen.

He set down his cup and said, "Yes, so am I. There is not going to be any more sneaking around being done by you. You are sixteen not eighteen, and you have to live by some form of rules. Going out in the middle of the night to meet God knows who is not allowed in this house."

"You don't get to give me rules," I said suddenly seething in anger.

"I'm your father. I get to do whatever I want when it comes to you. Don't ever forget that."

I stood up, placed my hands flat on the table and leaned in toward him. I was tired and cranky and not in the mood for his bossiness. "You were never my father, and you don't get to be him now. I don't take orders from you." I turned on my heel and tried to leave the room with my dignity intact.

It never fails that I apparently don't get to retain my dignity. My mother, pale, thin, and gaunt, stood in the doorway. Actually, she was swaying on her feet weakly, but there she was all the same. The anger and disgust on her face warned me of her mood. "Abigail! Apologize to your father right this second."

I hadn't seen her in weeks, well not for more than a moment, but that was the greeting I got. She looked sickly, really sickly. A soft breeze would knock her down, and I doubted she'd had anything to eat in days. Or maybe anything she ate that stayed down. I didn't want to upset her, but I was going to anyway.

"No," I said.

My father had come up behind me without me knowing. I'd been focused on how bad she looked that I hadn't heard him.

"It's all right, honey," he said soothing her. "What are you doing up?"

"I was hungry," she said with a laugh. She actually laughed. "I know, right? I woke up this morning just ravenous."

She reached out her thin hand to him and he quickly took hold. They shared a secret loving look that made me want to vomit and also made me severely jealous, but I didn't want to think about that emotion.

Just like that, I was invisible. My father walked my mother around me as if I wasn't even there and sat her down at the table. "Well then, let's get you something to eat!" He was almost shouting and the discernable joy in his words clutched my heart. I hated it.

He spun around and dug through cabinets and the refrigerator. He pulled out bread, eggs, bacon, and butter and went to town whipping up something for my mother to eat. I stood quietly by the wall and watched for a moment. They didn't acknowledge me at all. I slipped out the door and left them to it.

I stood in the hallway and tried to figure out what to do or where to go. I didn't want to go back to my room. I'd already spent too much time there. I decided to go see what I could find in the library.

I entered the dark room and sniffed the air. It smelled of old paper and leather. "Ah, now that is a good smell," I said. I didn't bother turning on the light. My eyes were able to see in the dim of the room. One of the perks of being a wolf.

I found an old book of poetry, which was not usually my thing, but I was in the mood for it that day. I settled into an old velvet-covered chaise and opened the book.

I didn't know how long I'd been there, but it had to have been some time when the door opened, rudely interrupting my quiet enjoyment. I didn't look up from my book; I already knew who it was. It was the sound of his steps and the smell of his preferred cologne that gave him away. "If I am going to be stuck in this house with characters from an old horror movie I'd at least like a little bit of privacy."

Derek came over and sat at the end of the chaise and said, "Always so dramatic. What are you reading?"

I slapped the book closed and tucked it next to by body, "Nothing exciting. What do you want?"

"I thought you'd like to know that the two clans are getting together for a formal meeting to discuss the Hunterz."

I sat up, my attention firmly on him. "Really?" My grandfather and my father had listened to me? Actually taken what I said seriously?

"Yes. The threat to your mother was the tipping point for your father. He is not about to take chances with her or the child."

"But I don't matter."

"Don't play the victim, Abby," he said and slugged me playfully on the arm.

"The victim?" I said and pulled away from him. "No one gives a crap if I'm threatened. But Lord Almighty, let a threat be made against my mother and the world has to come to a stop." I flopped back on the chaise and said, "This family sucks."

"I don't understand you," he said.

"Clearly," I replied.

He frowned at me. "You don't want to let anyone in. You don't want any help from anyone. Then you get mad when they give you exactly what you ask for. You wanted the other clan to be told of the trouble. They set up a meeting. Why are you pissed?"

"You're right – you don't understand me at all," I said. I pulled the book back out, opened it, and tried to go back to reading. Just because I pretended to everyone that I didn't need any help and that I could take on the world alone didn't mean I wanted to. It didn't mean I didn't want people to care. I wanted to matter. Why was that so hard for all these wolves to understand? I wanted them to give a shit about my feelings and me.

He stood up and stared down at me. When I didn't respond in any way, just continued reading my book, he sighed and left the room and me alone in it. Just like I wanted. Or was it?

Chapter Twelve

The wolf clan meeting was to take place on Sunday. They couldn't agree on a neutral place to hold it, so it was going to be in the middle of the forest halfway between the two main clan homes. One being my grandfather's and the other being William's home. And they said I was difficult. They couldn't even agree on a meeting place that was inside.

My grandfather and father were heading out the door for this meeting, and I fell into step behind them. My father stopped so quickly that I almost ran into him from behind. I leaned around to look up at him and said, "Dude?"

He apparently didn't like me calling him that because he frowned at me. Surprise, he didn't seem to like anything I did. "You are staying here," he said.

I was already shaking my head at him before he'd finished his decree. "No, I'm not. I'm going."

"No, you aren't."

"Um, yes, I am," I said right back.

My grandfather entered the un-winnable argument and said, "You will not be safe around so many of us right now. Plus, you are a girl." As if that made any difference.

I turned my attention to him and said, "I'll stand downwind. Regardless, I'm going." I didn't care what they said. They were not stopping me. Besides, I wanted to know what they planned and what was said at this meeting. I wanted to see how they acted around each other in this type of setting. Oh, yes, I was so going.

"Who will look after your mother and keep her safe?" my father asked.

Oh, he was hitting below the belt with that one. My mother and I were not in a good place, but I still didn't want anything to happen to her. "You said she would be safe here. If you are still worried about her, maybe you should stay home."

He blew out a harsh breath and turned to my grandfather as if to say, "You do something with her." Which is funny because my grandfather and I did get along. We had more of a relationship than my father and I did. He would back me up. I knew he would.

"Abigail, you will stay home," he said.

I swear my mouth fell open in shock and hurt at the betrayal. "You are supposed to be on my side!" I don't know why I thought that, but he just was.

He cleared his throat and looked uncomfortable. Good. It didn't sway his decision, though. "I am on your side, but this is not a meeting for females. You will stay home."

I clamped my mouth shut and ran upstairs to my room. I slammed the door with such fury I knew they heard it. I wanted them to know how upset I was. Not that it would really matter to them. I still wanted them to know.

I stepped over to the window and watched them as they left the house and walked out to the forest. I watched them until they disappeared in the trees and the darkness. Then, I left my room. I walked down the stairs, out the door and followed them, as I intended all along. "Keep me at home like some kept woman. I don't think so.

Who do they think they are?" I mumbled to myself all the way to the woods. Once I stepped into the forest, I became instantly quiet. I had to listen and use all my senses in order to follow them. I had a basic idea of where to go, but I also didn't want to get to close enough to my father and grandfather that they would sense me before we arrived. I didn't want to fight with them and have them try to send me back again.

It was sneaky, and I was surprised they didn't expect it. I had given up a bit too easy. I should have fought a little more, made it harder for them. Maybe next time, especially since I was certain there would be a next time.

I found them by scent. They were a good ways ahead of me and they got further away by the second. I smiled and picked up the pace. Running was so much more fun anyway.

We ran for a few miles. I knew I was close when I saw the light of a small fire up ahead. I slowed and circled quietly around to the other side. I didn't want my girl smell to give me away. I shifted over to stand within the trail of smoke from the fire to try to mask myself even more.

I tried to see who all was at this meeting of the clans. I could see William. Nice, he made it down for the shindig but didn't think to come and see me. Heck, he didn't even call, why was I surprised. There were Taylor and Jacob and across from him was…

Wow, a lot of families were there in force. Did they expect a fight? There hadn't been that many wolves together since my change. Maybe a meeting hadn't been such a good idea. It was too late by then to change any minds.

"Gentlemen," my grandfather said. He raised his arms and tried to get the crowd's attention. He wouldn't stay nice and docile for long. They better shut up if they knew what was good for them. I'd seen him in action.

I crouched down and focused on him in order to hear him better. Apparently, the others understood my grandfather or had at least heard stories about him as the mass of men quieted. "For the first time in decades, our common enemy has resurfaced." He let his words sink in before he continued. "We need to come together to fight off this threat. Most of you don't remember what it was like before. Death was all around us. The slaughter of our children was common. We can't let the differences between our two clans give them the upper hand against us. We can fight one another later. Right now, we need to fight together against the Hunterz."

Silence greeted his words. I thought it was a moving statement. I wanted to stand up and clap and cheer. Apparently, the others didn't. Low murmurs began to rise from the crowd. It slowly became a roar of noise. Everyone was talking to everyone. They were all giving their thoughts and opinions, their agreements and dissents.

It was complete and utter chaos, but even within that chaos, I could see the men were talking. Even better was that they weren't staying within clan lines like I expected. They were moving and mingling and discussing. It wasn't the chaos I thought it would be. It was a moving chaos that had a bit of hope in it.

Allan, William's father, yelled for quiet over the crowd. His face was lit by the fire. The old scar that ran along one side stood out in the light and shadows that moved over his face. As they had my grandfather, they quieted quickly and listened.

"I remember the Hunterz. They were here when I was just becoming a man. Until now, I thought they had been beaten down forever. I thought they were gone. They are only men, clouded by jealousy and by greed. It's a darkness that has eaten away at their group for a century or more. That darkness makes them uncontrollable and dangerous. It makes them evil. We must stop them. I don't want to see anyone hurt or killed. We don't know how big they have grown over the last twenty-something years. We need more information in order to be prepared." He looked at all the faces around him. He nodded his head once. I didn't know if it was to the people or more for himself, but his next words were said with a firm resolve. "The Greys are willing to work with the Statons, if they are also willing."

I snapped my attention back to my grandfather. Were we willing? I was, but was the rest of the group? Every eye in the crowd was now on my grandfather. He also took an inventory of the group. Then he raised one hand and said, "Yes. The Statons are willing."

It wasn't a cheer that rose. It was more ominous than that. The men, as if one being, leaned their heads back and howled into the night. There was no moon to call them. It was a joining. It was loud and powerful, both in force and in meaning. The two clans, separated for so many years, were coming together. Maybe it was only temporary. Maybe it was a beginning to better relations. Maybe it was just the lesser of two evils. It didn't matter. I saw hope in the joining. I saw a better future because of it.

No matter what the Hunterz were, they were the one force strong enough to bring the broken family back together. Even if it was only for a moment, it was a start. There was balance in the air, and it made me happy inside, where I had not been happy for quite a long time.

I stood up and decided to leave the group without the knowledge of my attendance. I had what I had come for. I turned and began a slow jog back to the house.

I wasn't paying any attention outward. I was too busy thinking in my mind about the joining of the clans. How I could use it to help me meet my own goal of getting the wolves to balance. Would rejoining the clans into one make that goal easier? Maybe if they weren't busy worrying about one another, they could work on that? Either way, I was enjoying the run back to the house until I crashed to the ground on my face.

I sat up, spitting dirt and leaves out of my mouth. I shoved my hair out of my face and looked to see what I had fallen over. I was surprised by the tumble because my wolf hadn't let me fall since coming out. My ankle hurt. Pain was pulsing from it, letting me know that I had done more damage than I first thought. "Ow," I said as I leaned over my foot to see how much damage had been done.

"Sorry about that, love, but it was the easiest way to get you down."

I snapped to attention at the first rumble of the voice behind me. I slowly turned my head to see who it was. I didn't know him. He appeared very tall from where I was sitting. His hair was blond, so blond it appeared white. His face was thin and angular with very showy cheekbones. His eyes were a light, piercing green, not the warm dark green of William's. He held a bow in his arms. Not an old, wooden type but a metal, lethal looking one. A compound bow, that's what it was called. I wasn't into that type of thing, but it looked big, dangerous, and scary.

"Umm…why did you want to knock me down?" I asked tentatively.

His lips spread into a wide smile, showing off his crooked, but very white teeth. "Easier to take you in if you are hurt just a little," he said.

I felt all the blood drain out of my face at his words. "Take me in? Where?"

"You'll see," he said as he whipped out a black canvas bag. It looked like a big laundry bag, but I doubted he intended to put clothes in it.

He headed toward me and I cringed backward. I started to reach for my wolf – she was stronger than I was, maybe she could save me. Something stopped me, though. He didn't have to say it, but I knew by the way he was dressed, all in fake leather and jeans, that he was part of the Hunterz. I wasn't about to give them any proof of what I could do.

134

"What are you..." Those were my last words before he swung back and punched me in the face, hard. I saw a snap of silvery light, and then nothing but darkness.

~ * ~

I awoke slowly. It was like my brain was drunk and sluggish. I became aware of my thoughts one piece at a time. Why was I on the ground? Ow, my ankle hurt. So did my face. What the hell? I could smell the forest, but it was different. What was that smell?

I opened my eyes and saw that I was not, in fact, in the forest. I was in an old barn type building. I was on the floor, but it was coated in what appeared to be cedar chips or animal bedding. Nice, I was being treated like a hamster. Lovely.

Then, I realized something more worrisome. My ankle was shackled with a big industrial sized chain that was affixed to a wooden beam behind my head. "What the hell?" I said. My words were loud in the silence of the empty...stall? I grabbed the chain with both hands and pulled against the wall. It didn't give an inch. I stood up, and almost fell back down. My one ankle really hurt. I gave it a cursory look, but other than the fact that it was bruised and swollen, there wasn't much I could tell or do about it in my current situation. I stepped gingerly under where the chain was hanging and again took hold of it. I pulled with the weight of my entire body. Nothing.

I inspected my foot where it was clasped in metal. It was like handcuffs, only wider. I tried to point my foot to make it smaller, but the cuff of metal was too snug against the bones and skin of my ankle.

If I shifted to a wolf, it would be smaller. I would be able to get free. But then what? There were no windows in the room. There was one door across the way. I picked up the chain so it would not drag on the ground and limped across the room to try the door. It was locked, as I had expected.

Should I bang on it? Call attention to the fact that I was awake? Scream and yell and hope someone would hear me that would actually help? I could shift, but would that do my people or me any good?

I knew who had me. I remembered the man in the woods. I knew the Hunterz had taken me. It wasn't hard to figure out. What did they want with me? I was under the impression they thought I was not a biological child of my father, so I wasn't of wolf blood. Even if I was the real child of a wolf, I was only a girl and girls didn't shift. They thought wrong on both accounts.

I crossed back to the far side of the room away from the door and sat down in the corner so I could keep an eye on the room. I was afraid. I could taste fear in the back of my throat, but I wasn't immobile with the fear. The real problem, aside from the captured thing, was that my head hurt, and because of that, I couldn't think straight.

I pulled my knees up to my chest and laid my head on them. Should I change? I could fight them better and the chain wouldn't hinder me as a wolf. However, I still wouldn't be able to breakout. In wolf form, I couldn't exactly open up doors. I would have to stay in this form until I knew what they wanted and how to get out. Once I had an escape plan, I could shift and run for it.

I sat for a while, alone with only my thoughts. At least with the bedding in the room, it didn't smell like animal. Above the pounding of my head, I heard someone coming in my direction. I could hear footsteps on the cement outside the door. They came closer and closer as they headed my way. My heart picked up speed and raced in expectation and fear at what or who would open the door. How many were there? Two? Three?

I heard the click of the lock then a loud squeal as the door handle turned. The door to my cage swung open fast with such force that it slammed against the wall and bounced back. Had the men not been standing there, it would have slammed closed again. Instead, one of their arms reached out to halt it mid-swing.

I slowly lifted my eyes from the big arm and focused on the faces. I was devastated to see that although one was the man from the woods who had captured me, the other was Brian. Brian, my once best friend, my once ally. He turned on me. Of all the people in the world, I would never have expected him to betray me. Never him.

"Oh, Brian," I said. "How could you?"

"It's for you own good," he said defensively.

I held up my foot with the chain hanging heavily from it and said, "Really? My own good?"

"Lucas?" he said, turning to his companion.

The one called Lucas didn't appear embarrassed or even upset. "We can't be certain she isn't one of them," he said. "It's for our own good as well as hers. We can't have her shifting and attacking us. They are evil and violent, and who knows how many she could kill if she wanted to."

"But you told me girls couldn't shift, that they didn't have girl babies. You said she couldn't be one," Brian said.

"You mean they lied to you, Brian. Say it isn't so," I said with such dramatic sarcasm that the words dripped in it.

He got my hint and frowned hard at me. "You aren't helping," he said.

"Good," I replied right back, my voice full of angry venom. "If my not helping screws with you guys, then I'm happy." I turned my stare to Lucas and asked, "What do you want with me?"

"We have our own plans, which are none of your business," he snapped. Then to Brian he said, "We have been going through the old texts, and there used to be girls. Not as many of them, even in the beginning when they were at their peak, but there were girls. We need to be sure she isn't one of the evil shifters."

"Geez, really?" I said rolling my eyes. "Evil? I suppose most adults think teenage girls are mean, but evil is taking it a bit far, don't you think?"

"Shut up," he said.

"Don't talk to her like that. You said she would be safe here. I never would have helped you if I thought she was going to be hurt," Brian said. His face was turning red with emotion.

"She is safe here. Look at her. What could she get hurt on? We are just going to keep her until the next full moon. She will have to shift on the full moon. They all have to shift on the first night of the full moon. If she makes it through that night without shifting, then we know she isn't one of them."

"He didn't say what would happen if I did," I pointed out. I wasn't really worried. I wasn't forced into the change like the others. All I had to do was wait it out. It was only…what, two more weeks until the next full moon. I could live with that, couldn't I?

Brian turned to face Lucas dead on and asked the question I had planted. "What will happen to her if she does shift?"

I smiled. Brian, God love him, was too easy to manipulate. I frowned as I realized that was what probably got him into the situation we were both currently in. I would have to work on that with him. Well, if I didn't kill him first when I got out of this mess.

Lucas smiled at Brian as well, but his was not the same as mine. His was dark and mean. "Then she dies, just like the rest of them."

Brian exploded into action. He dove at Lucas and screamed, "That was not what you promised! You said she would be safe here. You're a liar!"

Brian was not a big man. He was young and still not yet filled out like most sixteen-year-old men were. Lucas shook him off easily and threw him to the ground. He leaned over Brian and pointed a finger right in his face and said, "Don't!" Then he took a breath and said with forced calm, "She is safe here, for now. That's all we promised you. Don't mistake who we are. We are going to finish off this demon family. That is what we do. You knew what we were when you joined

138

us. She is part of that family. One way or another, she is part of it. Whether you like it or not."

"But," Brian said.

Lucas quickly cut him off. "No. That's it. She is either going to be with us or not. If you can't handle that, then you should leave."

Brian, still sprawled on the floor at Lucas' feet, looked at me and then at Lucas. "Will you promise she will be safe until the full moon? Then when she doesn't change, will you let her go?"

I stifled a laugh. God, he was an idiot. They couldn't just let me go. Whether I shifted at the full moon or not, they couldn't ever let me go. Safe and unharmed were also two very different things. He obviously didn't know that either.

"She will be safe here, as long as she cooperates with us," Lucas said.

See? Safe and unharmed didn't mean the same things. Not to me and not to Lucas. Brian, however, didn't realize it. "Okay," he said as he got back to his feet. "See, Abby? Everything will be fine. This is just for your own protection." He actually had the gall to smile at me.

He didn't really believe the crap he was saying, did he? I looked at Lucas. He and I knew the truth of the situation even if Brian refused to see it. He was too caught up in being a part of something. "Sure, Bri," I said. I could have told him the truth, but it wouldn't do him or me any good. He didn't want to see or know that he had pretty much handed me over to my death. Well, if I couldn't find a way out, that was.

"Go check in with the others, and let them know she is awake," Lucas said.

Brian, back to oblivious even though he'd just been knocked to the ground, was giddy and excited. "Sure," he said, "I'll run over right now." He turned, tossed a wave in my direction, and said, "I'll see you in a while, Abby. Don't worry. Everything is under control."

I couldn't bring myself to say anything back. I watched him walk away. His spine was straight and his shoulders were proud. I fantasized for a moment about knocking the holy crap out of him. It would seriously give me great pleasure to wrap my hands around his throat and squeeze.

In the distance, I heard the sliding of a door, presumably confirmation that Brian had left me, alone, with Lucas. He didn't have any sympathy on his face. He didn't see me as a girl or a human. He saw me as a scientist did a slide under a microscope. He stood leaning against the doorframe. His big beefy arms were crossed over his even bigger chest, and he stared at me. Studied me.

I hadn't moved a muscle since they had opened the door. I sat small in the corner with my legs pulled up close against my chest. I sat waiting as he stood studying.

Neither of us said a word for several minutes. Then, he dropped his hands down to his sides and came fully into the room, his eyes focused on me the whole time. Without looking back, he closed the door behind him. The sound of the door clicking closed brought immediate fear with it. I felt my body get hot and sweat begin to drip its way through my pores. My muscles clenched in trepidation of the unknown.

He walked slowly and purposefully in my direction. He stopped about a foot away from me and squatted down to eye level. He cocked his head to the side and regarded me. He reached out and I flinched back, knocking the back of my head against the wall behind me. He moved quickly and there was nowhere I could go or run. He knew it and was getting off on my fear. I could tell by the wide smile that spread over his face. Oh, yeah, he was enjoying it all right.

"Hey there, pretty girl," he said, running his rough finger down my cheek. I didn't flinch that time. I stayed perfectly still and watched.

140

That didn't stop him though from antagonizing me further. "You and me, we are going to play a game," he said. "I'm going to ask you some questions, and you are going to answer me."

"And if I don't?"

That sick smile returned for a moment before he answered me. "Then I will hurt you."

That was simple. Great.

He stood up and towered over me while he asked his first question. "Are you a wolf?"

"No." It was technically true. I was both a human and a wolf. I was not just a wolf.

I think he saw the technicality in my face as he kicked out at me with his booted foot. He didn't strike me hard enough to really cause any damage, but hard enough to cause pain. "Don't play with me, girl," he said. "Are you a wolf?"

I glared at him. I refused to show him that his little insulting kick hurt me in any way. Even though it stung, I didn't rub at it or even acknowledge I felt anything unusual. "No," I said.

"You and me," he said as he squatted back down in front of me, "are going to go at it one day."

I had a feeling he was very right. We were going to fight it out soon. The difference was I wouldn't be chained to a wall and trapped in a room. I also wouldn't be in this weak, human form. I'd be the wolf and I would tear his face off. Oh, yes, we were going to go at it all right.

Without warning, he slapped me across the face. One second, I was glaring at him the same way he was at me. The next, my face was on fire and my eye felt like it was going to explode. His explanation came in the growled words, "Answer me when I am speaking to you."

Oh, my God, my face hurt. My eyes burned with tears that wanted to be shed. Not so much out of emotion, but from the pain in my cheekbone and eye. I willed the tears to stay put, but they didn't listen to me. They dripped down my angry face without my consent. I said through clenched teeth, "You didn't ask me a question. You made a statement. One that I happen to agree with." I wanted to add a vulgar insult to the end, but I refrained. I was at his mercy for the time being. There would be time to get back at him.

"Man, girl. You have spunk. I'll give you that," he said as he stood up again. "Tell me about your family."

"What about them?"

He spun around and pinned me with his eyes. "The wolf part of them."

"I don't know any wolf part of them." I didn't know how to make him believe me or if it was even possible. He already knew all he needed to know about us. He just didn't realize it. I was going to try to keep him from realizing it. I also didn't want to antagonize him. It wasn't that I was afraid of him. Okay, yeah it was. He was big and angry and he could do some real damage.

"We'll see about that." He pulled out a big switchblade and slapped the blade open. The metal shined in the bright light of the one bare light bulb in the room. It winked at me as if it was laughing. I may not have showed it on the outside, but inside, I quaked at the sight of it.

Lucas strolled over and stood before me. "You know, I have heard that your kind heal quickly. Almost supernaturally fast."

"I don't know what you are talking about," I said emphatically. I truly didn't. "I'm human. I heal the same as everyone else."

"Let's find out," he said.

"No." I shrank back away from him. "Please, don't!"

He didn't give any indication of even hearing me. He grabbed my arm without any trouble, even though I tried to hold it against my body away from him. Then he sliced downward with his big shiny knife and slit open my arm in one quick motion.

I screeched in fear and pain and kicked out at him as I tried to pull my arm away. He swatted my feet away like he would have a fly and held my arm steady before him. Blood rose quickly to the top and began to drip down my arm to the floor between us. "Stop it! Let go!" I screamed at him

"Quiet. Watch," he said, his eyes steady on my arm.

My eyes were on my arm too, not in fascination, but in horror at all the blood. It was a lot. It ran and dripped fast without any indication of stopping on its own. "I'm just human!" I screamed as I pulled on my arm. "Stop it!" I was going to die. Reality told me I wasn't going to die from the one slice on my arm, but all the blood pouring out that looked like a river to me was enough to make me feel like I was.

He held fast for another moment, despite my trying to get him to let go. Then, when I was to the point of crying and begging, he growled and flung my arm away from him. I quickly pulled it in against my body and wrapped the hem of my shirt around it as tight as I could. "Idiot! Asshole!"

He shrugged, not annoyed at all. "Well, we had to find out one way or another, right?"

"Yeah, what I found out is that you are an ignorant douche!" I shrieked at him. Fear and pain loosened my tongue and made me careless.

He slapped my face again. Not as hard as he had before, but a little tap for effect. "Be nice," he said.

Right then I wanted to go wolf so he could see how freaking nice I could be! I didn't respond to his bait. He stood, turned away from me, and walked out the door. The turn of the lock on the outside was a loud sound that all by itself brought both relief and fear with it.

I looked down at my arm as I unwrapped it from my blood-covered shirt. It was a long slit about two and a half inches long. It was a clean cut, though. Smooth and fast, but it burned and pulsed with pain. It was also still bleeding. "Fast healers. What a freaking idiot." I wrapped it back up and held it close against my body to put pressure on it to try to staunch the blood.

Chapter Thirteen

After that, the day didn't get better for me. I sat alone for a long time. Silence was my friend. I had to be the only living thing in that barn. I reached out with my senses time and again, but there was nothing to hear or smell, other than myself.

After several hours, a new problem began to present itself. I had to go to the bathroom, bad. Thankfully, just as that issue came to a head, I heard movement outside my door. I stood up and waited for them to come to me. Since there was no other reason for them to be there, I didn't have long to wait.

The door swung open to allow Lucas and one other person into my room. "See. There she is, just as I promised," Lucas said.

I huffed out a breath in disgust. Did I come with a big red ribbon tied around my waist too?

The tall stranger didn't appear impressed. He scowled and squinted with his almost black eyes. I was a little surprised he could even see me, as his hair hung black and shaggy down over his eyes.

After his inspection and without ever saying a word or even really making a sound, he turned and left the room. Maybe I wasn't what he expected, or maybe I was. I turned my attention to Lucas, and it was a good thing I did because he tossed a bottle of water at my head. Had I not been looking, it would have hit me. Instead, I was able to catch it and glare at him at the same time. Then he tossed something else at me. It landed at my feet

I picked it up and looked at Lucas in disbelief. It was a processed jerky meat stick. Gross for anyone, but as a vegetarian, it was disgusting. From the look on Lucas' face, I had a feeling that was the point. Asshole.

He saluted me with a cocky smile and turned to leave.

"I have to go to the bathroom," I said.

He stopped, but didn't turn around. "So?"

"So? I have to use the bathroom," I said. What the hell?

He turned just his head to give me a look that told me I was not going to like what he had to say. I was right too. "What do you think the bedding is for in here?"

He had to be kidding. They did NOT expect me to use the floor as my own personal bathroom. Oh, my God. No, they didn't.

The horror must have shown on my face as he laughed and continued out the door. I looked around my room, wondering if I would be able to actually use the floor and whether or not I was going to have a choice much longer. Sooner or later, nature would take away my choice no matter what I wanted.

The door swung back open without notice and Lucas threw in a bucket. It bounced off the floor and came to rest at my feet. He pointed at the bucket and said, "One bathroom. Happy now?"

No. I didn't have to say it, though. He already knew it and probably expected it.

"Enjoy your night," he said as he closed the door. The turning of the lock was loud and made me feel hollow inside. As if things couldn't get any worse, a few seconds later, my light snapped out. It was a good thing I really was a shifter because without any windows or light, the room would have been pitch black. Thankfully, I was able to see in the darkness. There wasn't anything to see, though. It was still just a stall in an old barn with no windows and one door filled with hamster cage bedding.

I heard the two men leave, and silence again descended on my little world. I tried to wait as long as possible, but I ended up having to use the little pail for its intended purpose. It was disgusting and I didn't have any TP. I pushed the pail into one of the corners and then I curled up in the one furthest from it. I sipped on the bottle of water. I was thirsty, but I didn't know when I would get another. Also, the more I drank, the sooner I would have to use the pail again. Neither prospect was all that enticing. The meat stick, I didn't even pretend to eat. It sat unopened on the floor. I decided I wasn't that hungry yet.

The night wore on. I guess I didn't really know if it was night or not. It felt like it to my body, but without a clock or anything else, it could be afternoon and they were just messing with me for the fun of it. However, assuming it was night, it was long. I stood up and stepped over to where the chain was connected to the wall. I inspected it but didn't know what I was really looking for. I yanked, I pulled, and I twisted. Nothing happened. It stayed just as solidly planted in the wood as it was when I first arrived. I then paced the confines of the room. The chain allowed me to get to every space in the room except the far corner by the door. I was about a foot away from the wall of that corner. All the rest I had access too. I sat down in the center of my cell and looked at the circle of metal around my ankle. There was no closure or opening. It was as if they had sealed it around my ankle.

"They never intend to let me loose," I said. "I am going to die here whether I'm a shifter or not."

I needed to do everything and anything I could to get loose. I was not going to die in a little barn where no one would ever know what happened to me, except the lunatic Hunterz.

I sat and pondered the issue of my chains. If I shifted my foot to wolf, my leg should slip out easily. I focused on my foot and lower leg and allowed the shift to take over. It was surprisingly painful as my foot reshaped to form a thick paw and my leg thinned. It was enough of a change that the ring of metal around my ankle slipped down and over my foot without a problem. The foot that I had to shift was the one I had hurt running in the woods. Pain had emanated through my shifted leg. The change had rolled over the injured bones of my foot. I pushed aside the pain and put the ring back on. Then I shifted it to human. The circle of metal was tight and secure again, just as the Hunterz would expect it to be. My ankle pulsed with pain again for a few minutes before it settled back into an annoying ache.

I sat and contemplated my situation. When was a good time to do it? I could lay in wait for them, but the question remained of how to get out. There were always two people when they came. There seemed to be one to watch the door, and one to interact with me. Also, there could be more outside I didn't know about. I needed to really pay attention the next day. Try to listen and get a feel of how many came and left and what their schedule was. I could deal with one more day. I just needed to stay strong.

I lay down on the bedding. It tickled my skin and poked my face. There was nothing comforting about the chips on the ground other than their smell. I was suddenly overwhelmed with emotion. It was as if the act of lying down took away all my defenses and my emotions took over. I sniffed back tears, but they refused to stay back. I sniffed again, but all the fear and pain and sadness overwhelmed me anyway. As the tears refused to be contained and dripped down my cheeks, the wood chips stuck to my face and neck, making me feel all the more sorry for myself.

I did finally cry myself to sleep. I don't know for how long, but the sudden slamming of the door opening snapped me awake and into a sitting position. My wounded arm made itself known right away thanks to the ache and pain caused by the sudden movement and the pulling of the skin around the wound.

"Well good morning, my lovely," Lucas said. He was dressed in fresh clothes and his blond hair looked dark, as if it was still damp from a shower while I lay dirty on the ground in yesterday's clothes.

He didn't come bearing gifts of water or food. He marched over to me and without warning grabbed my arm and squeezed it hard around the barely healing laceration. I screeched in pain as he reopened it again and blood began to spill from the wound. I yanked my arm out of his grasp. Either he wasn't expecting it, or he had seen what he wanted to see and let go. Either way, I scooted back from him angry and in pain.

The man from last night, the stranger, poked his head in the door at the ruckus. "So?" he asked.

"So, no healing," Lucas replied.

"Duh!" I screamed at them. "I told you I don't have any super powers of healing!"

The stranger eyeballed me without expression and said, "And why would we believe you?"

I retreated further to the corner and put the wall to my back. I bowed my head. I didn't want to look at them. I had to stay strong in front of them, I knew that, but they were making it so hard. I was hungry and my arm hurt. At least my head and ankle felt a little better. My head was almost good to go, but my ankle, not so much. The phasing from the night before hadn't done it any favors. I needed that ankle to heal before I tried to run. I wouldn't get far if I were hobbling around on a bad foot.

I may not have looked at the two men, but I was very aware of their every move. The stranger had retreated back out of the room, and Lucas stood by the door. He headed in my direction. I was ready for him, though. He was not going to hurt me anymore. He wasn't.

He smelled funny. It was a musky scent that filled the room. My eyes flew wide and I zeroed in on his face. He was turned on. I could smell his arousal. I don't know how I knew what it was, I just knew. Fear flooded my veins. He wasn't simply walking toward me. He was stalking.

I gripped the chain in my hand. The metal felt cool against my hot hand. He came at me, with both hands outstretched. I don't know what I expected him to do, but I wasn't giving him the chance to do it.

I whipped the chain up and wrapped it quickly and tightly around both of his wrists. I yanked downward as hard as I could. I jerked so hard, my hands slammed against the floor as well. His arms and then body followed with a sickening slap. He grunted in pain, I hoped. With my good foot, I kicked him in the face. I watched with satisfaction as he flew backward and landed like a turtle on his back. His wrists were red and raw in a few places, which made me happy. I'd have been happier if they were bleeding as he had made me.

The satisfaction was short-lived. He rolled to his feet and glared at me with rage. He came at me again. He didn't care that I was half his size. He didn't care that I was a girl or that I was chained up and couldn't defend myself. His anger was all he saw. He slapped my face hard. My head whipped to the side and the bone around my eye cracked into the wall. It didn't end there. He stood and kicked my legs out from in front of me, which left my body exposed. I screamed in his face as he lunged. His body collided with mine and I was forced to the cold, wood-chip-covered concrete. His weight held me down. I punched and bucked, but it did me no good. He was too big and too heavy. He grabbed my wrists together with one hand and held them over my head against the ground. His face was inches from mine. We were both breathing hard and our breath mingled together between us.

"Get off!"

He smiled. He was enjoying the tussle. Even the pain part of it, he liked. He stuck out his tongue and ran it over my lips. I jerked my head to the side, but that didn't stop him. He just followed along the edge of my face instead. His tongue rasped against my skin and left a trail of slime in its wake. "You are disgusting," I said through my teeth.

"I kind of like you," he said. Then he bit me, hard, at my jaw line by my ear. I knew he'd left a mark even if I couldn't see it. I felt his teeth break through my skin just under my jaw. I felt a little pop as the skin tore, and a small trail of dampness rolled down my neck. Maybe it wasn't blood. It could have been his saliva. I wasn't certain at that moment which idea I liked better.

He licked over the sting of his bite and then he stood, brushed off his clothes, and left me alone in the room. I lay on the ground panting for several minutes. Partly out of breath, partly to keep myself from crying and showing them they were getting to me.

Finally, I sat up and crawled back over to the corner. I took several breaths. I cleared my mind and tried to stay calm. I couldn't, though. My body was shaking and my mind was in chaos. I couldn't wait. I had to get out. I had to.

I spent most of the day alone. It felt like hours and hours passed. I conserved as much of my water as I could. By the end of the day, I had to open up the meat stick and force part of it down my throat. I was so hungry, I couldn't hold back. I was bored out of my mind, too. I kept playing scenarios in my head on ways to escape. The only problem was that in the scenarios I had super strength, which in the reality of things, I didn't. I stood up and paced the room. My ankle was still in pain, but I had to either get it working enough to not slow me down or I had to get used to the discomfort. One way or another, I was getting out. My arm, most likely thanks to the constant reopening, was now angry red and looked to be getting infected, most likely thanks to the condition of my prison. It wasn't that it was dirty, but in the end, it was still a barn stall. Who knew what was in there before me.

When the door opened the next time, I was prepared for a fight. I didn't have to, though. The person at the door was Brian. "Get out!" I snarled at him.

Maybe I should have played him and used his sympathy to help me, but I was too proud and too angry to try it right then.

"I know you are mad," he said.

"Really? You have me kidnapped and tortured and you think I'm mad? Are you insane, Brian? I am way past mad," I said.

"They said you would say that," Brian said. He came into the room and sat down next to the closed door. Did he not know that I could still get to him there if I wanted to? My chain did reach that far.

"Say what? That they're hurting me? That they're starving me and have only given me one bottle of water since I was brought here? Did they tell you that?" I said.

"Yes. I know they are feeding you. They showed me the crates of food they brought in for you. They also said that you are hurting yourself. You have to stop that, Abby. I don't want you to be hurt."

I was dumbfounded. He couldn't see the truth. No, that wasn't quite true. He didn't want to see. If he did, he would have to admit my situation was entirely his doing. He couldn't have that. He saw himself as my savior, not the cause of my pain and eventual death. I saw the truth for what it was, he simply didn't want to.

"Go home, Brian," I said and buried my face in my knees and arms. I could try to show him my arm and even the bite mark on my neck, but what was the point. I knew that he would come up with some convoluted reason why and how I'd done it to myself. He didn't want to hear anything else.

He tried to talk to me, but I wouldn't respond. I wouldn't look at him or engage. Finally, he appeared to tire. He stood and knocked on the door to be let out. "I'll see you tomorrow, Abby." He said it as if it would reassure me, but all it did was make me sad. I would still be a prisoner when tomorrow came. Another day lost and wasted in the hellhole of a barn.

"Go to hell," I said within my knees, but I knew he heard me. He sighed and I felt the words he wanted to say, but didn't. Then he left me there, again.

That night my dinner consisted of a bottle of water and another meat stick. Where was my crate of awesome food Brian swore was out there just for me. He was an idiot. The night passed much the same as the last one. I paced the room. I worked on the chain. I practiced my shifting out of the ring. Then I cried myself to sleep.

In the morning, I awoke on my own without the door-slamming alarm clock that I'd had the day before. I used the lovely facilities. Then I settled back to enjoy a few sips of water and half a meat stick. "Oh, my life is grand," I said to no one, not even myself. I stepped over to the door and quietly tried the handle. Not that I was surprised to find it locked, but it would háve been a great happy moment to find it open.

I heard movement outside and quickly stepped away from the door. I backed up and almost fell over my pail. I glanced at it to make sure I didn't spill anything when my eyes locked on the bucket's handle – the little metal curvy handle. I lifted my eyes away from the hopeful weapon and turned them to the door just in time to see it open. Mr. Stranger stood in the doorway.

"You have a name?" I asked. It wasn't that I really cared, it was more the fact that I wanted to put a name to his face.

"Why do you want to know?" he asked.

I shrugged. "It's a human thing. Maybe you wouldn't understand that, being a demon and all." My sarcasm was not lost on him. He only showed it in the raise of one eyebrow, but I knew he got it.

"Todd," he said.

"Hmm, such a normal name."

"So."

"So I expected something like Damon, or Sateen. Something to match the evil I see in you," I said. I don't know why I was taunting him. I didn't really have anything to loose. They could make me suffer more, but I was dead either way unless I escaped. Besides, baiting him gave me something to do, and frankly, it made me happy, even if only for a moment.

I should have kept my mouth shut. I wasn't invincible, and I wasn't immune to pain. He was smart enough to know that when, apparently, I wasn't. He grabbed a handful of my hair at the top of my head and yanked it back until I was looking way up at him as he stood over me. "You are the evil in the world. Maybe you don't know it. Maybe you can't shift. But if you are of his blood, then you are as evil as the rest of them. You and your kind are nothing but animals with too much power. If I can take out just one of you, I will."

"So why are you keeping me here then? Just kill me and be done with it," I said through clenched teeth.

"I will learn everything I can about you and your kind before I kill you. I won't waste the opportunity that was handed to me." He smiled. It was worse than the usual dead look he carried on his face. It showed the crazy evil he was inside. Him, I was afraid of. Not because he was going to kill me, and I knew he would if I didn't stop him. No, it was because of what he would do to my family and my friends. I couldn't give him any proof of us. I had to make him doubt himself. I had to be strong and keep our clans safe no matter what.

"Todd." I intentionally used his name to try to humanize him, to try to humanize myself. "We, my family, aren't what you think we are. We're just people, the same as you. I know you won't believe me. I know you don't want to believe me, but it's all I can give you. I'm human. I'm nothing."

"We will see," he said. Then he left me alone in the room for the day.

I briefly wondered where Lucas was. He was usually my morning greeter. I almost wished he were there. At least with him, I understood his game and his plan. He enjoyed the taunting and the fear and the power. It was fun for him. Todd, I wasn't even sure he knew what his game was other than to kill and destroy. Insanity ran in the veins of his body, and it would only grow stronger.

154

Chapter Fourteen

The day was as long as they had been for the last few. I had nothing to do except sit with my thoughts and fears and plans. As promised, Brian did make an appearance in the afternoon. I assumed I was his after school chore. He entered the room. I stood up and hobbled over to the corner and refused to engage with him. As he had the day before, he sat just next to the door.

It bothered me. Why did he just sit there? I finally had to ask him. "Are you afraid of me, Brian?" I had interrupted him mid-sentence. I don't even know what he was talking about because I wasn't listening.

"No," he said. "Why would you think that?"

"Because you don't come into the room with me. You sit there safe by the door. Is that in case you need to make a fast exit?"

"No," he said again. "I am just giving you space."

"You do know that I can reach, right? If I wanted to hurt you, I could. They couldn't unlock the door in time to save you." His face suddenly lost its color. It made me chuckle. "I mean, if I am this wild half-beast creature you all seem to think I am, I could tear you apart in seconds, right?" I shrugged just to taunt him and said, "I'm just saying."

He stared long and hard and then pointedly looked at his watch. "I need to get home. My mom will worry."

That instantly set me off. "What about my mom? What about my family? Don't you think they're worried and upset and wondering where I am?" I stood up and stalked toward him, the chain behind me dragging the ground. It was loud and obnoxious in the background.

Brian scrambled to his feet and put his back against the door. He knocked loud and hard and frantic. I threw back my head and laughed. He was scared of me. Not just anxious and worried, but honestly scared. I swung out and slapped his face with my nails drawn. I watched in satisfaction as three angry red lines immediately appeared where I had struck and small pebbles of blood seeped out and slowly dripped down his cheek.

He smacked the palm of his hand against his cheek and yelled, "Let me out!"

I lowered my chin and looked up at him with as much menace as I could put into a look and said, "Don't come back, Brian."

The door swung open and he jumped through it. Lucas looked from Brian to me. He winked at me before shutting the door behind him and Brian. I stood, breathing heavy as I tried to get my temper under control. I heard Lucas as he taunted Brian, "Did the hellcat get her claws in you? I told you to watch out. She's feisty."

I couldn't make out Brian's reply. I didn't care. I didn't want to know what he thought or said. I dragged my chain back to my corner and sat down heavily on the floor. My belly growled in the quiet of the room. It couldn't be much longer before they brought me my water and my meat stick.

The little burst of temper cost me, though. I was so tired that day. Whether it was lack of sleep, lack of food, or little water, I was weakening by the hour. I wondered if that was their plan. Wear me down so I would be easy to get rid of. I glanced at the pail across the room. It shouldn't be long until lights out. I would see what I could accomplish once I was alone for the night.

Several hours later, the lights snapped out without warning. Wait, where was my 'dinner?' I stood up and hobbled my way over to the door where I pounded on it. "Hey! Did you forget something?" I shouted. I knew they could hear me, but I didn't get any response. I listened hard and heard the outside door shut. They'd left me and didn't even provide me my meager survival meal.

I kicked the door with my bad foot and regretted it almost immediately. It has started to feel a little better that day and I had just abused it. "Oww, frick!" I said through my pain-clenched jaw. "Damn it!" I hobbled over to sit down in my corner. I rubbed my ankle as best I could through the metal ring.

"Fine," I said. I dug through the sawdust and pulled out the last half of the meat stick from the day before that I had been saving along with the last of my water. I ate the meat stick and drank half of my water and saved what little was left for an emergency. I didn't know when my next meal would come or if one would come at all.

I let the small meager amount of food settle in my very empty and unhappy stomach and gave the people holding me time to get far, far away. Then, I set to work. I inspected the handle of the pail they had given me. It was a thin rod of metal connected to rings on opposite sides of a rim. It wasn't all that solid. The metal was thin enough that it could be bent, not easily, but bent all the same. I worked on unhooking it. I pulled and pushed and finally using leverage from the ring itself, bent the metal enough to get it undone. It sat in my hand, warm from my skin and the working of it to get it free. The ends were bent out of shape and it was sharp along the ends.

I reshaped one side so it was sort of straight. It was wonky here and there but not too bad in the long run. I crawled over to the door and looked at the handle and the lock. It was hard to see in the dark, but I made due. The door hadn't been there long. The wood didn't match the stall and wasn't as solid as it appeared. It kind of, well it sort of reminded me of a bathroom door. The lock wasn't great either. They must have had faith that the chains would hold me because the lock was pitiful. A household door lock. It was one that you could unlock easily if you had the right tool. I didn't have the right tool, but I had a tool, and I was going to give it a go.

I slid the metal piece from the pail into the small hole in the center of the doorknob. I twisted and poked and prodded to get the door unlocked. I tried and tried, but nothing happened. I got frustrated and threw the piece of metal against the far wall, where it fell onto the chips on the floor. I had to get up, get it, and try again. I used force. I used a soft touch. Nothing I did would fit the tip of the metal into the piece inside the knob to allow me to unlock it. I was ticked off at myself and angry tears were running unchecked down my face as I fought with the door.

Then, a sudden and unexpected snick of sound told me I'd gotten it. I stared in shock at the door as it opened under my hand. I did it. Oh, my God, I did it. I jumped to my feet and did a little impromptu dance, giddy with relief that I had done it. I set my lovely metal tool next to the door and began to work getting out of my shackle. I shifted my leg and was easily free.

I almost turned and left, but I stopped. I didn't want to leave any trace or possibility that I was able to shift into something other than a human. I was afraid that if I left the ring whole, they would know.

Without my ankle in the way I was able to work the metal. I twisted and bent it back and forth, up and down. I stepped on it, used my weight to flatten it down. I then could pull the two halves apart as far as I could before doing it all over again. Soon enough the metal weakened, and it broke in two. "There," I said very happy and proud of myself.

I jumped up and shuffled to the door. It made no sound as I slowly opened it. I peeked around the frame. It was as dark outside the door as it was inside. I looked right and saw a wall a few feet away. I looked left and saw the hallway open up. I really was in a barn. The doorways that lined the walkway were stalls with wooden sliding doors. Only the room that I was in had an actual frame and door on it. They'd gone to some trouble for me. Not enough, though, since I was about to make an escape.

I tiptoed down the hall. My hands were sweaty. I stopped mid-step. I thought I heard something up ahead. I craned my head forward and listened, hard, but heard nothing. Maybe it was a mouse or some other rodent. I sniffed the air to try to find out, but there were too many animal scents in the building. How long ago had the barn been in use?

I waited another second and then moved on. There was a door straight ahead. It was a pull to the side type of door. I reached for the handle and yanked as hard as I could. I was free!

The door swung sideways. There, in the dark of the fresh night air, stood Lucas. The shock and surprise evident on his face by his wide eyes and open mouth told me he was just as shocked as I was to find him standing there as he was at finding me in front of him.

I quickly took several steps backward as he came forward. "Hey!" he yelled.

I had a brief thought about shifting and making a run for it. That thought was quickly squashed as his body filled the doorway and blocked any chance of running I'd had. In a panic, I turned and ran the way I'd come. I didn't know where I was going to go, I just ran away from him. He chuckled and chased after me. I saw the haven of my cage and put on a burst of speed to reach the room. Not that it would do me any good, but it was the only place I knew.

Before I could reach the room, Lucas tackled me from behind. We fell to the ground. His weight on top of me pushed the air from my lungs. I smacked my forehead on the ground and stars circles my head like a Looney Tunes cartoon character.

159

I felt him sit up and I was suddenly flipped over and facing him. "Where you going, cupcake?"

I growled. I didn't plan on it, it just happened. The very animalistic sound vibrated out of my chest in warning. Lucas stopped for a moment. Then a very big smile bloomed on his face. "You going to go wolf on me, girlie? Come on, show me what you got."

I tamped down on my urge to tear him apart with my set of canine teeth. It was hard, and I almost couldn't help myself, but I did. I was not going to change for them. They were never going to know that I could do it. Ever. Instead, I bucked my hips up as hard and high as I could. Then I lifted my bent leg and rammed it into his crotch.

He gasped in pain and the smile on his face changed to one of pain. I smiled at him as he fell to the side off of me. I slipped out from under the dead weight of his legs and crawled away from him into my room. On my hands and knees, I shoved aside handfuls of the bedding as I searched in the dark for that little piece of metal I'd used to open the door. It was the only real weapon I had at my disposal. I just had to find it. I waved aside more and more sawdust and still couldn't put my hands on it. "Where the hell?" I screamed.

I looked behind me and saw that Lucas had climbed to his feet. He was a little wobbly on his legs, but he was standing and was spitting mad. Really, he had slobber dripping off his lips. I watched as a small bead gathered under his chin before it dropped to the ground and out of sight. He headed toward me. His hands were out toward me in claws and his face held a snarl of rage. "I am going to kill you," he said, and I believed him.

I crab walked backward as far as I could. My back hit something cold and metal and I realized I'd come up against the far corner where my pail sat. I reached out to steady it, not wanting it to spill. Then, I looked at Lucas again and back at the pail. I didn't have time to really think my idea through. Instead, I grabbed the pail, stood up and winged it right at his head, contents and all.

I missed his head, but it clipped his shoulder. I watched as it tipped and dumped and sloshed over his face and down his body. The smell of old urine and waste hit me first. I gagged at the sight and smell. Even though it was mine, I couldn't help but be overwhelmed and disgusted by what I had done.

The roar from Lucas told me he wasn't impressed either. He took one step and leaped at me. His full weight crashed into my chest and slammed me to the ground. My head hit the wall once, and when I hit the floor, my neck jerked back and my poor abused head hit once again. I saw a sharp flash, but stayed conscious. I wasn't sure if that was a good thing or not because Lucas was not done with me by any stretch.

He punished me without restraint. He kicked. He punched. He slapped. I curled up on my side with my back toward him and screamed at him to stop. I pleaded with him to stop. He either didn't hear me or was too incensed to care. He stood over me and enjoyed every painful moan he could elicit from me.

Then he stopped. I don't know what made him finish, but the torture simply ended. I heard him panting behind me. I didn't hear him squat down next to me. I only realized it when he grabbed a handful of my hair and forced me to look at him. "This is your own fault. You brought this on yourself," he said. Was that his way of apologizing?

I closed my eyes. I felt tears slip down my face and I know he saw them. Lucas had brought me to the brink of breaking. I'd wanted to be so strong. I wasn't though. I was just a young girl alone in a horrible situation. The only thing I held onto was that I hadn't shown them my wolf. I hadn't given anything away. It wasn't much, but it was all I had.

He let go of my hair and my head dropped back to the floor. I didn't move. I hardly dared to breathe. Everything hurt, even the rise and fall of my chest caused pain. He left the room and slammed the door behind him. I wasn't alone for long, though. When he returned, he came with the sound of jingling metal. I didn't need to see him to know what he was doing.

I heard the rasp of a match and the whoosh of a flame. That sound made my eyes fly wide. Then I smelled a chemical scent. I turned as little as possible to be able to see what was happening. It wasn't something horrible like I expected. He was soldering a second chain to the ring on the wall next to the other. He was quiet and meticulous as he worked with the flame.

When he was finished attaching the second chain, he turned to me and grabbed my feet. As I was curled tightly into a ball, hovering between pain and consciousness, the added jolt of movement through my harshly abused body caused me to cry out.

He didn't seem to care that he was causing me more pain as he clamped a ring around each foot. Then he brought the flame forward toward my feet. I flinched back and tried to pull away. His strength and my lack thereof gave him the upper hand as well as a firm hold of my feet.

I squealed in fear, expecting to be burned by the flame, but I wasn't. He ran a cloth under the ring before sealing them shut. Although I felt the heat, the cloth protected me from the burn. I stopped fighting, which was a relief, as I hurt everywhere. My head was swirling, and pain radiated through me all the way down to my toes.

Lucas was quickly done. He dropped my feet cruelly to the ground as he stood up. My heels crashed down with a thump, adding another layer to my already abused body. "Maybe this time, you'll stay where you're put," Lucas said.

He picked up his tools, kicked my bathroom pail back into the far corner of my room, and slammed the door behind him as he left. I heard an audible click as he locked me in. I crawled and slid my way over to my corner, where I finally relaxed and allowed myself the relief of sleep.

162

The next day, I was alone for most of the day. No one came in to check on me. No one came to give me water or food of any sort. I didn't move much at all. I slept most of the day. Not that it did me any good. The more I slept the more tired I seemed to be. I was severely dehydrated by that point. The one time I'd had to get up to go to the bathroom, there wasn't much to go, but it had burned and ached all the same. My head hurt, my body hurt, sleep was the one thing that helped mask the pain. My lips were cracked and the left side of my top lip was very swollen. One eye wouldn't open all the way. I gingerly felt my way around my face. I couldn't see it, but I knew I was in bad shape. My body wasn't much better. Aside from my stomach, which I had protected by curling into a ball during the worst part of Lucas' rage, the rest of me had to be one giant bruise. I winced as I tried to take in a deep breath and decided I maybe had a few unhappy ribs in there too. Broken or cracked, they hurt like hell.

I shifted my weight enough to change positions and then fell back to sleep for a little while. When the lights went out for the night, I knew I wasn't getting anything to eat or drink that day either. It was my punishment for trying to escape. I lay in the dark for a little while, with my belly hollow and growling with hunger. I needed to figure out what to do next. In the shape that I was in, I couldn't think of anything except the pain, my hunger, and the thirst.

I tried to open my eyes the next morning when I heard the door fly open and slam back against the wall. They didn't want to cooperate. I think one was swollen shut and the other was sealed with tears and gunk. Nice.

I hissed in pain as I tried to sit up. I felt at a disadvantage lying on the floor as I was. I wasn't able to sit, though. A full day and then some since Lucas and I had our little clash, and I was so sore and in so much pain, I just couldn't do it. I did, however, peel one eye open enough to see that it was Todd that entered my quarters.

He obviously did not have one ounce of compassion in his body. He grabbed my head by my hair and yanked it up so he could see my face. "How did you escape?" he demanded.

My tongue felt big and floppy in my mouth. To make matters worse, it kept trying to stick to the roof. I didn't answer fast enough apparently as he shook my head as if to get my attention. He had my undivided attention, trust me. Then he asked, "How did you get out of your chains. How did you get out of the door?"

I couldn't tell him the truth. There was a part of me that wanted to. I was tired of hiding and fighting these men. They were nothing but pain and torture and I wanted it all to just end. Then I thought about what they would do to other wolves like me, and I couldn't bring myself to hand the knowledge over to Todd or Lucas. I couldn't bring myself to turn on my family and the clans. I was going to die anyway, no matter what I told them. So I'd die on my own terms.

"The chain gave," I croaked. Holy cow! Was that my voice? It was gritty and dark and nothing like I normally sounded.

Todd shook me again and demanded, "The door! How did you get out of the door?"

"It wasn't locked," I said. I kept the smirk off my face. If he believed me, then someone, Lucas, was in big trouble.

He let go of my head and I tried to make my muscles take hold, but they were too weak. My head flopped back down on the ground. My brain, I swear, rattled around in there with the shock of it. I could have killed for a tablet of ibuprofen, just one.

He didn't ask or say another word. He left me alone in the room again. I said a little prayer for water. I begged God for him to come back and give me a sip of water. I didn't even care if it was a whole bottle, just a taste, anything. God let me down, though; Todd didn't come back.

I cried, but there were no tears to show for it. Dry sobs sounded in the room. I didn't care if they heard me or not. Coming to terms with your own death is not fun. I knew it was coming and there was not one thing I could do about it. Would anyone miss me? Would my father or mother mourn or would they be happy? I wallowed in sadness for a long time. I didn't have anything else to do.

Later that day, when the door opened, I expected it to be Todd or Lucas, but it wasn't either of them. It was Brian. I didn't have to see him to know. I knew his smell, the beat of his walk, and the sound of his breath. My back was to him, and I didn't try to turn and face him. What was the use?

"Abby?" he called out.

I didn't answer.

"Please, talk to me," he said.

"Why are you here?" I croaked. "I told you to leave."

"I know," he said. "Why won't you look at me?"

"Go away," I said. I was too tired to talk to him or anyone.

I heard him get up and walk over to me. His steps were slow on the used and stale bedding that littered the floor. I opened my one good eye when I sensed he was almost in front of me. I was not disappointed in his reaction. I must have looked even worse than I thought I did because he gasped and took a step back. "Oh, my God! What happened?"

As if he had to ask. There was a part of me that simply wanted to close my eyes and not answer him at all, but then the other part of me said that I needed to try to get him to help me. "These people aren't what you think they are, Brian, or what you want them to be."

His face closed down. He didn't want to hear me. If he actually listened to me, then he would have to take part of the blame. I could see it in his face, even before I said another word.

I had to try, though. At that point, he was my only hope, slight though it was. "Please," I said. My throat was so dry it was hard to talk at all.

"They didn't do this to you," he said. "You're lying."

I wanted to beg for water. I wanted to beg for food. Most of all I wanted to beg him to believe me and to help me. "You know I'm not," I said instead.

"No," he said. He shook his head frantically and stepped away from me. "I don't believe you."

I took what energy I had and turned to keep him within my sights. "You don't want to believe me. Please, get me out of here. Tell my family where I am. Find my mom. Please, Brian."

"The shape changers are the evil ones. Not us. Not the Hunterz. You're lying!" he shouted. "I…I saved you. They were going to kill you. They were going to…"

"Stop it," I said softly, but he heard me and listened all the same. "You know that isn't true. This is the truth. Look at me and see it. These friends of yours, the Hunterz, are going to kill me. Whether you want to believe it or not, they are going to."

He shook his head again. "I don't believe you. I don't."

He wasn't going to help me. I flopped back to the ground and closed my eyes. If he wasn't going to help me, then I needed to save all the energy I could for myself in case I needed it. In case I saw a chance to run. In case I had to fight.

"Abby," he said.

I didn't move. I wanted him to leave. I couldn't bear to see him or hear him. Not being friends anymore had been hard to live with the last few months. Knowing that he was willing to risk my life for those men, for people he just met, and refused to see their lies no matter what I said or what he actually saw was burning my heart like acid and tearing me apart.

"Abby?" he tried again. I concentrated on breathing in and breathing out. I listened to my heartbeat. I did anything I could think of to tune Brian out. He must have gotten the hint as he knocked on the door to the men outside and said, "I'm ready."

I didn't open my eyes. I didn't see him leave. I didn't say goodbye. I heard him leave, and that was almost as hard. The knowledge that he left me there, even after all I tried to say, even after what he had seen with his own eyes, he left me, alone.

I was going to die. The full moon was coming. I couldn't stop or hold back the moon any more than I could get Brian to help me. I would die well, though. They would never know what I was. They would never see me for the animal I could be. They would always wonder, and I would go to my grave without giving them the answer they wanted.

"Fine," I said to the empty room. "Let's do this." I was ready to die, but I would take some of them down with me. One way or another, I would draw blood and leave my mark on them.

Chapter Fifteen

Time passed. I don't know how much. Was it hours? Was it days? I slept all the time. No one came to see me. No one came to give me food or water. It couldn't have been days, right? How long can you live without water? How long can you live without food?

Silence was my companion. I hardly ever heard any noise outside my door. Had they left me to rot? Did they not even want to see me die, just come back and find my corpse to be buried? My thoughts were morbid, and yet…where was everyone, anyone?

It was almost as if they heard my thoughts because soon thereafter, I did hear movement outside, lots of movement and the sound of many feet. That could not be good. I had moved over to my preferred corner and laid facing the door. I didn't move or sit up. I just decided to pretend to be asleep. It wasn't much of a stretch at that point, though. I had virtually no strength or energy. I was beginning to think that was the plan.

The doorknob turned slowly, almost as if they were trying to be quiet. After their stomping down the hallway outside, I'd have had to be dead to not have heard them coming. The door inched open. A tuft of brown hair eased around the door, then a forehead, and finally an eyeball, wide and watching.

I had my eyes almost completely closed except for a small slit that I used to watch. I concentrated on my breathing. I kept it steady and even. My heart was beating fast. It was a bit of a struggle to keep my breath calm and even, but I forced myself to do it.

The eye vanished as it snapped back out of sight. Then there was furious whispering behind the door, most likely to figure out what to do with me now. Idiots. I couldn't fight them by that point, especially since there was more than one person to contend with.

What were they doing? Get on with it. Whatever it was.

Even though I knew they were there, my heart still leaped when the door suddenly flew open and slammed against the wall. I didn't show it on the outside, but on the inside, the noise had taken me by surprise. The only outward show of movement was my eyes. I couldn't fake being asleep with that racket going on, but I could fake not being afraid.

And fake it I was. I was shaking to my bones. What were they going to do to me? How much would it hurt? Could I stay strong? Would the wolf force her way out to try to protect us?

Five men piled into the room. They were all like Lucas in shape: big, burly, and built like a truck. They were related in some way. Their blond hair was close in color, although not exact. They had the same eyes, both in shape and green tint. The rest of their faces had their own personal flare to them. One had sharp cheeks, high and prominent. One had a very, I mean very, large nose. Maybe it had been broken once or twice. The third had deep-set eyes and a dimple in his chin, deep and wide. I knew the other two. Todd and Lucas came in last behind the others. I should have expected them. I should have known. They were there in front of me in all their strength and bitter jealousy. No matter what they tried to call it, they were jealous of the wolves. That was why they wanted to destroy them…us.

I pretended not to care. I sighed loud and annoyed, then closed my eyes. Not quite all the way, I could still see them, even if they didn't know it. Maybe they did know it and just didn't care.

Everyone but Todd stood beside me. Todd stayed by the door. Then, they all grabbed an appendage. Lucas was up by my head with my left arm firm in his grasp. He ran his thumb over the long angry slice that was still evident on my arm. It was red and swollen and painful to the touch. It was very infected by that point, thanks to the unclean nature of my cage.

They hadn't been rough at that point, but as I hadn't been moving all that much after the tussle with Lucas, my muscles and my body were very sore. It hurt a lot to be pulled out of the small ball I'd stayed in. Every muscle protested and I gasped and hissed in pain as they held me out spread eagle in front of Todd.

I wasn't all that concerned since I was dressed, but being helpless was scary. Maybe that was the point.

"Not much to look at anymore, is she?" Todd said.

Lucas' response was a grunt. Did he agree? Did he even care? Did I?

"Skinny," Todd said.

Duh, that's what happens when you don't eat for days. How many days?

"I wouldn't get too cocky, man," Lucas said. "She's feisty."

"You would know," Todd said. The others chuckled at their own private joke. Only it wasn't private. I knew what they were talking about.

"Almost bested you, didn't she?" Todd asked. He tossed the words out at Lucas but never once did his gaze waver from me. He was intense.

More chuckles came from rest of the men. Lucas didn't respond, but his grip on my wounded arm grew uncomfortably tight. I tried not to react. I tried to tell myself it was only pain. Just like any other feeling, it wasn't any big deal, but it didn't work. I gritted my teeth and tried to hold back the tears, but they burned their way forward in my eyes and dripped quietly down my cheeks.

"How long until the moon rises?" one of the others, the big-nosed one, asked.

"Soon," Todd said. I didn't know how he knew. He didn't glance at a watch and there was no window to gauge the time.

They stood next to me for what felt like forever. No one moved, or hardly seemed to even breathe, and that included me. What were they waiting for?

Todd growled. My gaze flew to his face. It was a noise of frustration, but what took me by surprise was that he sounded almost animal-like. Not entirely, but enough to get my attention. Wait a second...I stared hard at him. Then the moment was gone. Nothing happened.

He stared at me and I stared at him. I wanted to ask him who he was, really, but I didn't. He was smaller than the others in the room, but he seemed more dangerous. His eyes were empty. His face showed no emotion. He was the most dangerous in the room. It would be smart to remember that.

His eyes squinted at me and his stare intensified. It was so hard I could actually feel the weight of it. The guy with the chin who was sitting by my feet sighed. "Anything? How long is this going to take?"

"Maybe she needs to be outside, in the light of the moon," Lucas said. It was actually a good idea. If I could get them to take me outside, then I had a better chance of escape even in my weak condition. It wasn't time for the full moon yet, was it? It couldn't have been that long.

"It could also be her clothes," he added.

My attention shifted from the moon to Todd then to Lucas in a heartbeat. My clothes?

"Maybe we should remove them," he said.

Over my dead body would they take my clothes from me. I had very little left at that point, but the protection of my jeans, filthy tank top, and bloodstained shirt were one of them.

Todd shrugged with such uncaring that I wanted to poke out his eyes just to see if that would get a reaction out of him. "We can try that," he said.

A smile of such disgusting excitement bloomed on Lucas' face. He turned to me and said, "I told you before that you and I would go at it, remember?"

I didn't answer, but I remembered all too well that conversation. I hadn't thought this was what he meant, though.

"Let's get her undressed boys," Lucas said to the other three holding me down. My shirt was quickly dispatched by a sharp pull from Lucas. There wasn't even time to fight him over it. However, the moment a hand reached for the button of my pants, I knew I had to fight. I didn't even stop to gather energy. I just reacted. I bucked and arched hard.

Lucas laughed as I came to life with aggression. He was enjoying the moment.

Butt chin was nice enough to think me weak. His hold had not been as tight when I buckled. He dropped my leg that he'd been holding. I didn't think at all when I pulled that leg back and kicked him as hard as I could in the face with the ball of my bare foot. The chains didn't hinder me even a bit. I felt his nose crunch under my big toe. He dropped to the floor and cradled his face in his hands, sounds of pain and anguish leaking through his fingers.

"You bitch! You broke my nose," he said from within his cupped hands over his face.

Maybe he would look more like big nose than he'd want to. It was a small, spiteful thought, but it made me happy all the same. Lucas and the guy with very sharp cheekbones clamped tightly on my arms. The guy with the big nose tried to contain my other leg, but I had leverage then.

I kicked up off the ground with my free leg and tried the same tactic with him as I had on butt chin. He was expecting it and batted my foot away with his forearm. He may have been expecting my move, but not the force of my kick, and I knew I hurt him when I connected with his arm and he hissed in pain. I was using all my strength, human and animal alike, to get free. I was strong. I was fierce.

It was not enough. Butt chin had regained his feet, uncaring of the river of blood pouring from his nostrils. He took hold of my flailing foot and took the upper hand, or foot, in this case, away from me in one single moment. I was down, but I was not out, and I wasn't giving up. I head butted backward. I didn't care who I hit with my skull as long as it did damage and as long as I connected. I did, but not with very much force. Lucas barked out a laugh and said, "Keep fighting, wild cat!"

I wanted to tear into him. I was not a cat – I was wolf, and I would devour him if I could only get the opportunity.

"Stop!" Todd bellowed. The word bounced off the walls and echoed around the room. We all stopped and turned to look at him. I didn't have much choice as I was good and tightly held down again. The problem was the moment I quit fighting, all the strength and power I'd held and used flowed out of me like water over a dam. My arms and legs went limp, and my head that I held up to see Todd suddenly felt so heavy and full that I simply could not hold it anymore. I wanted to give up and just go to sleep. I was again very aware of my thirst. For a moment, that discomfort had been pushed to the back of my head but again it was in my face with my tongue, thick and fuzzy, stuck to the roof of my mouth.

I let my head flop back and closed my eyes. I had to conserve whatever energy, strength, whatever I could because if an opportunity presented itself, I had to be ready. I didn't really believe that, but it gave my mind something to think about besides the pain in my body and the idea of being stripped down.

"Hold her down," Todd said.

The four men did as they were told. I felt their grips tighten. I didn't need to open my eyes to know they were intent on the job. I tried to stay relaxed, but I didn't know what to expect from Todd and my body clenched up whether I wanted it to or not.

I was expecting pain and torture. I was not expecting a gentle caress on my stomach. My eyes flew open and landed on his face. He was staring not at my face but my body. My tank had ridden up in the scuffle and the warmth of his finger gliding over my bare skin gave me the chills, and not in a good way.

A rumble of warning sounded in my throat. It didn't warn him at all. In fact, a smile played around the corners of his mouth at the sound. He flattened his hand full on my tummy, my aching empty tummy. Then he turned his eyes to mine. With sarcasm dripping from the words, he said, "Did you say something?"

I narrowed my eyes and said simply, "Don't."

"Or what?" he replied.

I didn't have to respond. In the silence of the room as Todd and I had our little standoff of wills, I heard something. Something very slight and quick to be silenced, but I'd heard it all the same. It was the sound of paws on concrete. Not so much the paws themselves, but the scrap of nails on the pitted floor.

My heart skipped a beat. Was it only my mind and my desperate hope or had I really heard what I thought I heard. I didn't have long to wait. A stream of wolves filed through the door. Eight? Nine of them? My little cage was filled to bursting at that point.

Lucas called out a warning to Todd when the first furred head came into view, but it was too late. A wolf, dark and big, pounced on Todd from behind and took him down to the floor. The rest of the wolves didn't stop to watch. They paired off and took out the men at my four corners, and I was instantly dropped to the ground.

My eyesight was fading in and out. Even with all the action going on around me, I wanted to close my eyes and sleep. I didn't care anymore whether I woke up or not, I was so tired and my body hurt so much. It was partly from the bruises, cuts, and possible broken bones. It was also from lack of water and food. I was starving to death and my body was eating itself to try to stay alive.

Then the smell hit, metallic and wet. The human side may have wanted to sleep and close it all away, but the animal came alive at that scent. My eyes flew wide, and my head turned left and right to find it. Derek, the black wolf on Todd, had ripped open his throat and blood poured out onto the ground in pulses that slowed as I watched. Todd was dying and I didn't care. All I cared about was the red pool on the floor.

I didn't give a thought to the men in the room. I didn't give a thought to maintaining my secret anymore. I had a feeling no one would make it out of the room alive anyway to tell my tale. My body shifted and changed. What was normally a swift and painless morph from human to wolf, was slow and full of sharp, intense pain. My bones and muscles were weak and half-starved. The change was not easy and I paid the price of the neglect from the past weeks. I shrieked in both surprise and pain. If anyone noticed, I didn't care. How long it took, I don't really know, but it felt like forever.

"I knew it!" Lucas cried out. "I knew I was right!"

Those were his last words as I stepped out from the bondage of the chains I'd been trapped in. They fell to the floor with a heavy jingle and I didn't think of them again. Maybe Todd said more, maybe he cried out in pain. I didn't care. He and I had finished the little game he insisted on playing and I'd won. Not on my own, but in the end, I won all the same. Two male wolves pulled him to the ground. One tore out his leg up by his groin. The other took out his throat. It was quick and I assume mostly painless. He deserved more pain than that.

Once the change was complete and I was in full wolf form, the pain was quickly forgotten and the call of the blood returned full force and with a desperate need. I crouched down, stretched out my neck and reached for the wet pool with my tongue. With the first touch and taste of it, everything around me turned red. My heart squeezed in my chest, and I lost total control of myself whether human or wolf, I was crazy with a need so fierce all I could do was give in to it.

I pounced into the small but steady growing pool of red. I flopped down into it, as I lapped it and drank it. I felt myself growing stronger and fiercer. Anger and rage built within me as I drank my fill of the blood on the ground. Part of my mind knew what I was doing and that it was wrong, but the wolf part just laughed and continued to soak up the precious red liquid.

I was nudged from the side by a wolf of soft brown. I knew the wolf, but at that moment, I didn't. I curled defensively and snarled at him. The well of red was mine and I wasn't sharing. I snapped at him. I growled and snarled.

I was out of control, but my body was so needy and hungry for anything. The brown wolf lowered his head and whimpered at me. He was trying to calm me. He was trying to reach me.

No! He was too close. He wanted to steal from me. I leapt onto him and clamped my teeth down into the soft fur and flesh of his shoulder. Warm blood, fresh and salty, dripped into my mouth.

176

Before I could enjoy the moment, I was ripped from his back and tossed to the ground. Derek stood strong and demanding over me, where I lay on my side panting with more emotion than I could process. He was outlined in a red haze. He lowered his head and growled loud and angry in my face.

I lifted my head and growled right back. The scent in the room was overpowering. It grew heavier and heavier. My mind was chaos and whirling in the scent. When I tried to rise and get back into the mess of it, I was pushed back to the ground. Derek was angry. Even within my mess of a mind, I was able to process that much. Even so, he was gentle in his control. He held me down with his front legs. Then he sat on me. His body flopped fully on top of me and held me to the ground.

All around was death and blood and I couldn't get to any of it. I couldn't sink my teeth into any of the men even though I wanted to. I wanted to tear them apart and make them pay. I wanted to cause pain and I wanted them to see me as I did it. I tilted my head back and howled at the injustice of it all. I wanted to be in the fight. It wasn't fair.

I closed my eyes and tried to breathe through the rage and the red. The blood smell in the room was making me crazy. The anger inside of me made it all the worse. A rough tongue ran over my nose. My eyes flew open. Derek was inches from my face and his eyes told me he understood. I twisted and tried to get up, but he stayed put, firm and heavy on my body.

He may have understood, but he was not moving. I closed my eyes again and settled onto the ground in defeat. I was crying inside, relief and impotent rage combining to cause the emotion. I shifted back to my human form and allowed myself to cry on the outside too. Not much in the way of tears were produced as I was dehydrated, but one or two found their way out all the same.

The warmth of Derek's body as he continued to lie on me calmed me more than any words could have. I didn't care that I was lying in a mushy pile of blood-soaked cedar chips. I didn't care that I was naked and surrounded by wolves. I didn't even care that along with the wolves were five dead men, all their throats torn out. The room was a massacre, painted in red.

The nine wolves were dripping. Their snouts and paws covered in blood. They didn't shift forms. They sat and waited for me to calm or to settle or who knows, but they were waiting. Derek slid off my body. He stood, next to me and tossed his head to the door, as if to tell us all to move out. Even in the den of death and murder, he was in control. He was a leader and they all listened to him regardless of who they were or what clan they may have been from.

As my mind cleared, I began to see who they were. It was my friends from the Grey clan and my new school lunch buddies from the Staton side. They'd come together to save me. My heart melted.

When all eight of the wolves had left, Derek moved from my side. It was then I realized he had been shielding my naked self from the others. Even in the wreck of the moment, he'd protected me.

I stood up and took one last look around the room that had been my prison. The walls were splattered and the floor littered with bodies. I stepped over to Lucas and stared down at him. His eyes were open but empty. The green that once looked like emeralds was dull and lifeless. There seemed to be a small smile on his face. It broke what little control I had regained. I kicked him with my bare foot. I stomped on his chest. I dropped to my knees at his side and slammed my fists down on his chest again and again and I screamed in rage and anger and hurt. I screamed until my voice was raw. I fell over his body that would not know of my abuse and sobbed. Derek stood steady and silent at my side.

178

When I was done, I rose up on shaky legs, lifted my eyes toward my freedom and walked out of the room. I didn't look back. I didn't need to. Derek stood at my side, my dark guard. My protector. I stalked down the hall toward freedom. The door stood open and wide before me. Outside I saw trees and green. I shifted quickly, although still a bit painfully. I walked to the opening and stood for a moment upon the threshold. I scanned the area, but it was empty of everything living. The others had run, content with the knowledge that I was safe and the threat had been removed. I looked over my shoulder and my eyes connected with Derek. He nodded once. I didn't need to say anything, he already understood.

When had we become more than enemies? When had we become friends? I didn't know exactly, but we had. Somewhere along the way, we had.

I shot forward and ran for the trees. Derek stayed next me. I was free.

Chapter Sixteen

"How did you find me?" I asked Derek. "At the barn, how did you know I was there?"

A few days had passed since my rescue. Between my father's yelling, which I was learning wasn't so much about anger but fear, and my mother crying, which I think was from hormones, and the steady, almost studying look, from my grandfather, my life had been strange since my escape. One thing I learned, though, was that they all did seem to care. Maybe they didn't show it the way I wanted them to or needed them to, but they did care.

"Brian," Derek said. We sat on the back step of my mother's house, facing out toward the forest.

"Brian?" I asked. No way.

"Yup," he said. "He showed up at your school. Being human made him stick out as it was, but luckily one of your friends noticed him and asked what he wanted."

"What happened?" I asked.

"He was lucky to make it out of there alive, actually. Mr. Staton, the gym teacher, locked him in the equipment room."

I wasn't sure I wanted to know the answer, but I asked anyway, "What is going to happen to him?"

"He has been made to understand that there is no such thing as shapeshifters," he said, only he didn't look at me when he said it.

"But…" I started to ask, knowing there had to be more.

"He was beat to a pulp for turning you over to those butchers. As I said, he's lucky."

Brian had saved me. Yeah, he was the reason I'd been in that situation to begin with, but he'd saved me in the end. I felt a smile form on my lips.

"What are you smiling for? There is nothing to smile about," Derek said. His face was one firm frown from his eyebrows to his mouth.

I shrugged. "It's just nice to know that he cared enough to put himself in danger to try to save me. I got through to him and he saved me."

"No, I saved you," he said and puffed up his chest in a show of strength.

"Yes, you and eight other friends," I said. Then I leaned over and placed a kiss on his cheek. "Thank you for coming for me." After a moment I added, "I don't think I would have lasted much longer."

"I don't want to talk about it," he growled.

No one did. My grandfather and father had demanded to know what they'd done to me, but the moment I began to tell them, they would yell at me that they didn't want to hear any more. They couldn't listen without getting upset. Yeah, they cared about me after all.

My friends had surrounded me with caring since my return, every one of them, all except for William. There had been no sight or sound of him. I didn't want to dwell on it, but I couldn't help it. The thought kept coming back to me time and again. Why hadn't he called? Why hadn't he reached out?

"Okay." I ran my hand over my hair. It was a mess, but it was finally clean. It had taken several showers and I had shampooed my hair repeatedly to get the smell of that cage out of my nose and off my body. I hadn't been able to look in the mirror the first night. What I saw while in the shower was enough to tell me I didn't want to know. My body was one big bruise from my head to my toes. Really, even my toes had bruises on them.

One of the clan doctors came to check me out and fix me up. My father had called him. They wrapped my chest and told me that although I'd suffered a few cracks in my ribs, they were not broken as I'd feared. They felt just as bad as if they had been broken, though. The rest of my body would heal, and it was, slowly. My mind, though, was having a harder time.

"You look better today," Derek said, changing the subject.

"Liar," I replied. I knew how I looked.

Derek was again watching the forest and not me when he asked, "Still not sleeping?"

I shook my head. Nights were bad.

He nodded that he heard or maybe that he understood. "It will get better," he said as if he knew it to be true.

I didn't know any such thing, but I went ahead and agreed with him. "Yeah," I said.

"Want to go for a run with me?"

I looked out at the forest, the place I had always found solace in. The place I had felt safe and happy in. Not anymore. There was danger within those trees. There was danger everywhere now. The forest looked dark. The trees as they swayed in the breeze looked evil. They smiled and waved at me and called me over to where they could get me. I shook off the chill that raced down my spine. "No," I said. "Not today."

"I'll be with you," he said.

"I know. Just not today."

"When, Abby?" he asked. "You can't hide forever."

"I'm not hiding," I said.

He was silent next to me. His thoughts, however, were loud and clear. 'Yes, you are,' they said. Even though he didn't say them with his voice, I heard them all the same.

We stayed that way until the sun began to set and the darkness stretched its shadows toward me. They stretched across the backyard, reaching for my feet. They passed the old swing set. They were coming. They were coming. I stood up quickly. "I better get inside."

"Where it's safe?" Derek asked, his eyes still on the forest.

I looked at the forest, too. It was calling to me as it was to him. The difference was he heard the caress of the trees and the hunger for the run. I heard the evil, the pain, and the terror that lived within the forest. "Yes, where it's safe," I said.

We had taken out five of the Hunterz. How many more were still out there? Todd wasn't the leader. He was only the son. He may have been next in line, but he was not the leader yet. There were still more out there and they were coming for me. They were coming for us all.

I stepped inside the screen door, gave one last glance toward the forest, and then I turned away from it. It was going to be another long night.

About the Author

Courtney Rene lives in the State of Ohio with her husband and two children. She is a graduate and member of the Institute of Children's Literature. Her writings include magazine articles, short fiction stories, several anthologies, as well as her young adult novels, A Howl in the Night and the Shadow Dancer series, published through Rogue Phoenix Press. For a complete listing, visit www.ctnyrene.blogspot com or feel free to contact her at:

ctnyrene@aol.com.

Also Available
by
Courtney Rene
From Rogue Phoenix Press

Shadow Dancer
Book One in the Shadow Dancer Series

Sunny has a gift that she has no idea how to use, until she meets Leif, a boy from the kingdom of Acadia, on the other side of the shadows.

Leif teaches Sunny about Shadow Walkers and how to use her new found gifts. As they grow closer and their gifts grow stronger, a threat arrives. The Shadow Guard has been sent to bring Sunny back to Acadia, to determine if she is a threat to the king as the rightful ruler of Acadia.

As Leif and Sunny prepare to defend themselves, Sunny finds that Leif has also been sent to bring Sunny back to the kingdom but for very different reasons. As a battle for possession of Sunny wages, she is struggling to come to turns with her feelings of inadequacy regarding controlling her gifts as well as the hurt regarding the lies and deceit of everyone around her.

An Excerpt

Prologue

"My Lady? I don't know what to do. I don't know what else...I think we need to call for help."

"Where is she? I can't see her."

"She's fine, my Lady. She's sleeping, right over there. Can you see her?"

"Bring her to me. I want to hold her."

"My Lady, you have lost too much blood. We need to get you to a hospital or something. Please."

"Star, it's already too late. You know it. We can't call for help. We have to keep her safe. She's all that's left. She is worth that and so much more. God, I am so tired. Please bring her to me."

"My Lady..."

"Even now Star, after all these years, can't you just be my friend?"

"I will always be your friend, my Lady, but you will always be my Queen. Even now, even later, that will never change. Here she is. Do you have her?"

"I've got her. Please don't hover over me, Star. I'm alright. Look how beautiful she is. Can you believe Malcolm and I made something so beautiful?"

"Yes, I can. She looks like you. She has your hair, all golden and soft. She has your mouth too. Don't you think?"

"Yes. Oh God, I want to hold on to her forever. I never want to let her go. Star, you have to promise me that you will keep her safe. Whatever you have to do, you have to keep her safe. Promise me."

"No, my Lady, we will keep her safe. You and I together."

"No, Star, this burden will fall to you. You already see the truth of it, right here in front of your eyes. I'm just so tired. Here, you'd better take her. Bye, my baby girl. I love you so.

Star, promise me. You've done all you can here. All that is left is her. Malcolm is gone, and I..."

"Stop it! You can't just give up! Don't laugh! Can't you see that it's tearing me apart? I can't do this without you."

"Star, I'm not laughing. I promise you. There just isn't anything I can do to stop it. You can do this. I believe in you. Star?"

"Yes. My Lady?"

"Promise."

"All right. I promise I will do everything I can to keep her safe."

"Do you think you will ever return?"

"I don't know. Everything is changed now. Our whole world has changed."

"Star?"

"Yes?"

"Stay safe. You have always been my very best friend. I don't know what I would have done without you. Thank you, so much, for everything."

"My Lady..."

"Keep her safe..."

Chapter One
Into the Light

My eyes snapped opened at the buzz of the alarm. Ugh, I could feel the distant thump in my head telling me a headache was on the way. I slammed my hand down on the clock to shut off the alarm. I threw my arm over my eyes and groaned aloud. Another Monday of my life in the eleventh grade, front and center before me.

Five-thirty came much too soon, especially since I didn't get to sleep until after eleven the previous night. I groggily sat up and swung my feet over the bed, stood up, and went to shower myself awake.

After my shower, I stepped in front of my closet to decide what to wear. Unless you are a sixteen, almost seventeen, year old girl, you just can't realize what a difficult task that is. I settled for a pair of black skinny jeans, a pink t-shirt over a light blue tank top. I finished it off with a black pair of flip-flops. As for my hair, I brushed it out, gave it a scrunch, and let it air dry from there. My one real beauty is my hair. It's long and golden blond, with soft flaxen curls.

With a soft touch of make-up on my very pale face, I was set to go. I scrunched up my face in the mirror. No matter how much time I spend in the sun, I never acquire that summer tan others flaunt. I didn't burn either. I just stay, as I always was, ghostly white. With a shrug of my shoulders and a last look in the mirror, I grabbed my school bag and went down to breakfast. That was as good as it was going to get for the day. I sat down at the kitchen table, dropped my bag to the floor at my feet, and I put my head down on my arms.

"What's wrong, Sunny?" my mother asked from where she stood in front of the burbling coffee pot, empty cup in hand, impatiently tapping her nails against its rim. My mother is my complete opposite in appearance. My eyes are a deep rich blue, and my mother's a dark chocolate brown. She keeps her shiny black hair short, in what we call a witch cut. I jealously noted that she still had her golden-brown tan, even though it was late October and the tanning days had been past for at least six weeks. It just wasn't fair.

"I've got another headache coming," was my mumbled reply from deep within the depths of my arms. The thumping in my head was growing increasingly more persistent. It did not bode well for the day.

My doctor said the headaches are part of puberty, except, news flash, I had hit puberty three years ago and the headaches had only begun about four weeks back. They had come with a vengeance and seemed to hit more often and with more intensity each time.

"Did you take the medicine Dr. Backus gave you?" my mom asked. She set her cup on the counter and walked to where I sat. She gently pulled my face up from where it lay and took a good long look. I could never figure out what the heck she was looking for when she did that.

"Mom, you know they just make me feel like I'm gonna barf. They don't even make my head feel any better. I just get the added bonus of feeling sick to go with thinking my head's gonna explode."

"Maybe you should just take a day off," she said. "Stay home. You haven't missed any school yet this year. You could just be worn out."

I sighed quietly. It was October. How much time could I have already taken off? School had only been in session for about nine weeks. "Mom, I'm fine. If it gets really bad, I'll come home." My mom gave me that look again. "Mom really, it's fine. I'm good."

I loved my mom, and my dad, but sometimes it felt like they may as well have just rolled me up in bubble wrap and locked me away in a padded room somewhere. They hovered and coddled, and held on so tight sometimes. I was sixteen, not three. I was old enough to make my own decisions. Try explaining that to my mom, though.

In order to give my mother some small bit of comfort before I left, I put on a big fake grin, hefted my bag onto my shoulder, and with a happy breezy wave, headed off on my morning walk to the high school.

Frankly, the short one-block walk to school was excruciating. Maybe I really should have just taken the day off. It was a lovely fall day, but with every step jarring my head, I didn't take much notice. The morning sun was blinding in its radiance. With my eyes squinted into slits and my head down, I trudged on.

My day did not suddenly get better once I reached school. Not that I thought it would. I made my way through the throng of people to my locker. No one stopped me in the hall, no one shouted or said hello, and I doubt anyone even looked at me seriously. I hated being the new kid at school. It seemed like I was always the new kid. We moved around a lot, and it felt like I attended a new school every single year of my academic life. It seemed like I would just get settled in, make new friends then suddenly we were packing up and heading off to a new town or new city. I had lived from the warm summers of Georgia, to the cold winters of Washington State, and everywhere in between.

We had moved to the small town of Nelsonville, Ohio in early August, just in time for me to start my junior year of high school. When I say small town, I happen to mean small town. Granted, it has more than one traffic light, but not much more. The population of Nelsonville is about five thousand people. That should tell you something. It should also tell you that it's not easy to fit in here. If you weren't born there, you weren't part of the inside group. I had been making progress, but it was slow going.

I can honestly say I'm not sure how I made it through the day. I didn't remember much at all, except for the increased thumping and throbbing of my head. The day was worthless, lunch was inedible, and finally, at one o'clock, I gave up and called home. My mom picked me up, thank goodness. I couldn't have walked home. My head was fuzzy and my stomach was rolling with nausea. Any light seemed to just make it all worse. I dragged myself up the steps and into my room, dropping my jacket and bag on the floor along the way. I fell onto my bed and curled into a ball. My head was thumping, my stomach was heaving, my mouth was dry as cotton, and my legs were feeling weird and tingly.

I pressed my head into the soft mattress with my eyes tightly closed, trying to find some type of relief. I wanted the pain to stop. I needed relief, any relief. The usually refreshing scent of laundry detergent sent my stomach rolling again. I quickly turned my head away from the bed and breathed in through my mouth.

The thumping was drowning out everything. I felt like I was suffocating. I wanted to just escape it all. I wished desperately I could just sink into the bed to get away from the pain for a little while. The thoughts were like a mantra in my overburdened head. "Just away, just away, just away," I panted in a whisper.

Maybe I was dying. Maybe my head really was about to explode. "Just away, just away." The chant seemed to be working, if only a little bit. It was then that I began to notice a strange feeling. It wasn't just my legs that were tingling, but my whole body. I realized that I was blanketed in cold. There was also a subtle hum in the background. I didn't know if the hum was an actual sound, or if it was coming from me.

As I lay there trying to figure out what I was feeling, I heard my mom ask from outside the door, "Honey, are you all right?" Too engrossed in my own pain, I didn't answer.

"Sunny?" I heard my mother ask again, with a note of confusion in her voice. I eased one eye open to watch as she came into my room and looked around. It was just a standard teenagers' room. There were several pieces of clothing strewn about and make-up and hair supplies on the counter by the mirror. I hadn't opened the shades that morning, so the room was a bit dim, but otherwise, nothing out of the ordinary.

"Sunny!" Her tone was more anxious now, so I pulled together enough energy to sit up from the tightly curled ball I had been in on the bed.

"What?" I asked.

My mom swung around and stared at me in surprise, her brown eyes so wide that I thought for a moment she was frightened. But then her face softened and the tension drained away. "Oh, you startled me. I didn't see you there."

She gave a self-conscious giggle, which made me give her another look, but the fact was, even though the pain seemed to be receding, it was still quite intense, and I was wiped out. I just didn't have any strength left in order to try to figure my mom out. At least the weirdness I had been feeling had disappeared. In fact, it had left almost as suddenly as it had come. The cold was now gone as well as the hum.

My mom walked over to the bed, reached out and laid a cool hand against my cheek, then asked, "Should I call the doctor? You look really bad."

That didn't make me feel any better. Nothing like hearing you look like crap along with feeling like it.

"No, just sleep," I replied flatly.

"Maybe I should just give him a ring real quick," my mom continued, but I cut her off with a weak wave of my hand and a tired protest.

"Mom, sleep is all I need right now. Can you close the door on your way out?"

I didn't know if my mom left right then, or even if she closed the door on her way out, because my body had finally had enough. I closed my eyes, shut out the world, and thankfully went into a numbing blissful sleep.

~ * ~

When I woke up the next morning, I was feeling great. I glanced at the clock and realized I still had fifteen minutes before my alarm even went off. That was a true first. I was one of those people who actually needed eight to nine hours of sleep every night. Without it, I was a bear and a grouch all day long. Trust me.

I hopped happily out of bed, danced over to the window, drew open the shades on the still gray dawn, and enjoyed the sight. Afterward, I showered and dressed for the day as usual and out my door I went, bounding down the steps and into the kitchen. "Hey," I said happily as I met my mom in the kitchen.

She still had a fuzzy, sleepy look about her as she stood in her favorite ratty blue robe and wild hair. "Hey, yourself. I see you're feeling better."

"Much. I'm starving though. Do we still have bagels?" I rummaged around in the cupboard. Finding what I was looking for, I broke it in half and put it in the toaster. I then turned and leaned up against the counter to wait for it to pop. My mom was looking at me. "What? Do I have something on my face?" I asked, gently sarcastic.

"No," my mom replied, "but last night was a real doosey. You went to sleep and I couldn't wake you. I tried to get you to come down for dinner, but you just wouldn't wake up."

I finally looked at her, you know, really looked at her instead of just watching her while she talked. She had dark circles under her eyes, and she looked old for the first time that I could remember. There were lines of strain around her eyes I hadn't noticed yesterday.

"Mom..."

"Don't 'mom' me; I think it's time to go back to the doctor."

"He said they would pass."

"I think he should check you out." She continued on as if I hadn't said anything.

"He already checked me out just a week ago."

My bagel popped, and I watched without surprise as my mom walked out of the room. I sighed. Just once, I would have liked to actually win a discussion. I can't call them arguments, as whenever my mom or dad made a statement, they would just walk away, assuming their decree will be obeyed. I shook my head, knowing there wasn't anything I could do about it.

I smothered my bagel with cream cheese, wrapped it up in a paper towel, grabbed my bag, and left for school. The glorious day of an hour ago seemed diminished somehow.

I walked outside into a crisp fall morning. The sun was shining brightly, valiantly trying to warm the day. Before I even made it to the sidewalk, I became instantly alert. The hairs on the back of my neck stood up in attention. I felt someone watching me. I glanced around, and there, two doors down, in front of Mr. Shaw's house, leaning against the trunk of an autumn-leaved maple tree, stood the most gorgeous guy I had seen in a long time. *Ooh la la*. I took a moment to look my fill from under my eyelashes. I didn't want him to realize I was gawking at him. He had long, lean, muscled legs encased in worn black form-fitted jeans. He had slim hips and broad shoulders. The t-shirt was plain dark blue, but it fit nicely over his sleek body, showing off the raw muscle underneath. "Wow," I whispered under my breath.

When I finally made it up to his face, my steps faltered briefly. He was not smiling in welcome. In fact, he didn't have any expression on his face at all. He just stared directly at me. He was very nice to look at. His skin was clear milky pale. His lips were full but at the moment, did not look soft and inviting. Maybe they would if he was smiling. His cheeks were sharp and prominent. His nose was small, and, well, cute actually. But his eyes...holy cow, they were striking. Ice blue. Not cornflower, or sky, but cold white blue. His hair was black, down to his shoulders, where the ends curled up slightly. He needed a trim, as it was looking a bit shaggy around the edges, but it did not detract from his looks. It just gave him an edge of danger. Again, I thought, he was gorgeous.

As I drew even with him, I gave him a bright friendly smile that he did not return. That made it a bit hard to strike up a conversation. He just continued to look at me without expression. It was disconcerting, to say the least. I didn't know what to do. Should I say hello, or just look away and walk on pretending to ignore him? Boys are so strange sometimes.

Before I could make up my mind, he reached out and grabbed hold of my arm.

"Hey!" I exclaimed, trying to pull my arm free.

He held on easily. Leaning in close to my face, he looked me dead in the eye and said, "I know what you are."

Shadow Warrior
Book Two in the Shadow Dancer Series

Sunny finally makes her first jump to the Kingdom of Acadia that is on the other side of the shadows, for what she hopes is a vacation. Only her vacation turns into quite an unwanted adventure. Aside from new and unexpected issues regarding her relationship with Leif, Sunny meets the rebel group, makes new friends, fights with controlling her powers, and finds herself neck deep within a county that is torn apart by two sides, each fighting for power. Acadia is not quite what she imagined. How is she, one young girl, supposed to unite the Kingdom as well as unseat a King to take her place as ruler of Acadia.

Shadow's End
Book Three in the Shadow Dancer Series

The adventure and the struggle continues for Sunny, as the fight for control of Acadia is near. Battle lines have been drawn, not just by King Gideon, but also by the rebels that were once Sunny's allies. Due to unexpected trips to the ice realm and the fire realm, new allies are found to help build the Army of the Sun. There are new worlds explored. New friends and new enemies made. Ready or not, Sunny must prepare for what is coming as well as decide where she belongs within it all. But…what about prom? What about Leif? What about home? How can she, just a seventeen year old girl, rule a whole world? She's not even sure if she can get through finals.

Shadow Fire
Book Four in the Shadow Dancer Series

No one really knows who Leif is. They know the man he portrays and the things he has done, both good and bad. He was a boy that came from nothing and grew into a man full of rage that almost killed the one person he set out to save. He roams the realms waiting for death. Waiting for an absolution that doesn't come. Then a rumor surfaces. A threat has been made against Sunny. Leif sets out to try to right the wrongs of his past. He sets out to do what he was meant to do from the beginning, save the queen. Can he do it alone or will he have to do the one thing that is hardest for him, which is: Ask for help.

A Howl in the Night

Sweet Sixteen is supposed to be a turning point in your life. The world is before you in all its glory, just waiting for you to reach out and grab it. Right? For Abigail Staton no, not so much. Not only does she suddenly lose her best friend due to a fight, but suddenly her mother expects her to believe that the father, she has never met, is actually a werewolf. With that revelation, Abby is thrust into the world of two wolf clans who are not only fighting each other, but also fighting for Abby, one of the few females born to the shape-shifters. Her father is determined to pair Abby up with Derek, a very dominant and overwhelming shifter. Abby vehemently balks at this union to disastrous results. When war is declared between the two clans, Abby has to decide what side she is actually on.

www.ingramcontent.com/pod-product-compliance
Lightning Source LLC
Chambersburg PA
CBHW071603180626
46819CB00002B/110